Burning Love

Burning Love

A Hot Aussie Knights Romance

Trish Morey

TULE
PUBLISHING

Chapter One

CALEB KNIGHT SLAMMED his locker door shut and slumped onto the nearby bench, letting his aching head flop into his hands. Sometimes life just sucked, though ironically, that seemed an honour reserved for the witnesses – the ambos and emergency services who were first on the scene. Along with the family, of course, the ones left behind. The ones whose lives hadn't just been prematurely snuffed out because of some stupid, senseless, and ultimately fatal act.

He closed his eyes but he knew the images would stay with him. There was no way he could unsee what he'd witnessed today.

Like the images of the fifteen-year-old unlicensed and unrestrained driver, her long, blonde hair matted with blood, the fear she felt when she'd realised the two cars would collide preserved for all eternity in her open blue eyes as she lay broken and lifeless on the bitumen.

And of her cowardly nineteen-year-old boyfriend reeking

of alcohol and protesting to the police officers questioning him that it had all been her idea to drive, and that it wasn't his fault.

But then the gut-wrencher, the female driver of the other car trapped and barely clinging to life in the small hatchback that had been crushed like tinfoil when the high-powered Subaru had run the red light. Even the Jaws of Life he'd wielded hadn't been strong or fast enough to cut through the wreck in time to save her life, before her heavily pregnant body had been rushed to hospital in a desperate mission to save her baby.

Yeah, sometimes life sucked.

What a fucking mess. He sighed as he rubbed the back of his neck. He'd joined the fire brigade to put out fires, not to scrape people off the road. Although that was only half true. He'd joined because, going back three generations, that was what the men in his family did. From saving people and property, their pets and livestock from fires to demonstrating to the public at the annual Royal Adelaide Show how to use a fire extinguisher. And, sure, rescuing the odd kitten stuck in a tree. God, how he wished today had been all about rescuing kittens.

"That was a rough one," he heard Richo say behind him. "I sure could do with a cold one after that. You in?"

"Maybe." He nodded to get rid of his crew mate, to make it look like Caleb was on the same page, but he knew what he needed when he felt like this wasn't a day off. It was Ava.

He needed Ava.

Chapter Two

AVA MATTISKE SENSED the change in light behind her. Sunset, she registered with surprise, turning her head towards the big picture windows that ran one length of her studio and overlooked the steep creases of the Uriarra Gorge below to the city and sea beyond. It had been mid-afternoon the last time she'd looked out, the cloudless sky had then been an infinite blue, the air almost shimmering in the thirty-plus temperatures. Now the rugged gorge with its rocky escarpments and bush-filled slopes and ridges was alight with the golden red rays of the westering sun.

Her favourite time of day.

She turned back with a critical eye on the unfinished still life she'd been working on for days now. She'd been struggling to capture the poetry of the simple composition of lemons and blue and white striped jug she'd arranged against a snowy white-tiled backdrop. She thought she almost had it at one stage today, thought she could get it if she just persisted. But still it didn't sing with the vibrancy it should. Something was missing.

The light summoned her back to the windows, demanding her attention. There was no rush to finish her work, she decided, wiping her hands on a towel. No need to fight when she could finish the painting tomorrow. Right now it was the sun's turn to paint. She cleaned her brushes, poured herself a glass of chilled sauvignon blanc, and pulled up a chair on the terrace outside to enjoy the show. The sunsets were just one more reason to love living here in this special place in the Adelaide Hills, where the sky went on forever and the land was richly textured, the ridges and valleys steep and rocky, and in stark contrast to the long flat plains of Adelaide below.

She could never live down there on the flat. Texture was what she craved. Big sky. Shifting clouds. The sunsets were a bonus, just like the visiting wildlife, and the gully winds at night that came to banish the worst of the summer heat.

Not to mention the isolation.

She could work here. She could relax and let the ever changing landscape and the ever changing colours feed her soul.

She was safe.

Her glass was near empty, the sun a molten ball dipping its toes into the sea, when she heard a car approaching the house along the long driveway behind. She stiffened, cocking an ear, wondering at the intrusion. Caleb's car, she realised, and a momentary spike of pleasure at his unexpected arrival was tempered by the knowledge he'd broken the rules. In the time they'd been seeing each other, they never dropped by without phoning first. They never intruded on each other's lives without first checking it was okay.

He knew that.

She sat there, waiting, in the dying rays of the sun, wondering what had changed that he would do this and risk what they had, thinking she'd miss him if it had to end.

But then, it had been a while.

Maybe too long.

Maybe it was time…

She heard his footsteps crunch on the gravel driveway, and then he was there, standing awkwardly in the half-light, as if knowing he'd crossed some invisible threshold.

"I'm sorry," he said, his voice unusually thick. "Rough day…"

And suddenly she didn't need an explanation to understand because his stumbled words and his tortured eyes told her all she needed to know. "It doesn't matter," she said with a reassuring smile, as she stood and wove the fingers of one hand through his.

Because, even in the fading light, she could see the torment that was etched in his face and feel the pain that had brought him here. She pushed herself higher and pressed her lips to his.

It didn't matter that he'd broken the rules, not this one time.

Not when she knew how to fix him.

THEY DIDN'T MAKE it to the bedroom. They didn't make it inside. Her kiss was the trigger that unleashed something inside him, something untamed and wild. Primal. He growled and tugged her to him, his fingers tangling in the hair behind her head, his hot mouth meshing with hers, his tongue urging hers into the dance. She felt the knot at her nape come undone and the heavy tide of her hair roll down her back, while his hands – his big, beautiful hands – followed it, palming their way down her spine and lower, his long fingers squeezing the cheeks of her behind so she tingled with the press of his fingertips so close to her heated core.

A flock of black cockatoos screeched their way across the darkening sky as the light around them shifted, the colour leeching out of the day as he rocked her hips against the swell of his erection. He made a sound low in his throat, half a guttural cry of desperation half an admission of need, and then his hands were working at her clothes, frantically pulling at the buttons of her painting shirt and shrugging it over her shoulders and letting it fall to the ground without letting his mouth lose hers.

Her naked breasts firmed in the whisper of warm evening air, her nipples tight buds even before his hands found them. She sighed in his mouth as he cupped them, tweaking their aching tips, before his hands skimmed down her belly to find the snap at her waist and wrench the zipper, and her shorts and underwear were down before he began shedding his own clothing.

He was like a blind man, a man lost in a dark room and searching for the light. Or a diver out of oxygen, desperate to reach for the surface before his lungs exploded. He wasn't like the others. He didn't need her entertainment or her flattery. He just needed to be inside her.

And as she let herself lose her shorts and her sandals, she knew all she had to do was to be there until the storm passed and the tension in his body that was bending him into knots was gone.

She felt herself pulled into his arms again, his seeking cock colliding with her belly, as his tongue plunged deep in her mouth, his fingers clenched tight in the cheeks of her ass as he lifted her from the ground and spun her around towards the studio. The sunset-warmed glass met her back as he pressed her against the glass, wrapping her legs around his waist, her arms around his heated neck, while his hot tongue swept circles around her nipples and his erection pressing hard and insistent at her slickened entrance, until she was swept up in the whirlpool of sensations, and she whimpered with the conflicting pleasure and pain of it.

He didn't make her wait. His hands on her hips, he drew her down his length, each inch adding to the delicious fullness, and she shuddered at the sheer bliss of the connection.

His tortured eyes collided with hers as he lifted her slowly upwards.

"Ava," he ground out, as he held her there momentarily, before he surged upwards at the same time he pulled her down hard. "Ava."

He was like a storm unleashed after the calm, wild and savage. Elemental. But even as he thrust into her, even as her blood turned to mercury in the rush of heat from that delicious friction, that look in his eyes sent that cold lick of fear down her spine again. This was not how it was between them. This wasn't how it was supposed to be.

The realisation faded, increasingly blurred and indistinct until it was snuffed out by the sensations unfurling and blossoming inside her, sensations building as wave after wave of pleasure rolled through her, taking her with them, higher and higher. Until there was nowhere left to go, nothing there to hang onto, and one final powerful thrust of his hips launched her over the brink, and sent her spinning through a universe of sparkling lights in a velvet sky.

Gradually the shudders subsided as she floated back to her world, her ability to detect detail returning. Bit by bit she became aware of her pounding heartbeat, of his fractured breathing, and of the puff of his hot breath against her heated skin; the whiskers of his jaw that rasped against her skin where he rested his head in the crook of her shoulder, his fingers uncurling from her flesh as she unwound her legs from his waist. Tentatively, she tested her land legs. Her knees wobbled but didn't buckle. This was good.

He lifted his head and pressed his hand against the glass

behind her head, peeling his body from hers, the balmy night air rushing in to fill the void, whispering cool caresses over her scorching skin.

Then he leaned back in, kissing her softly on lips now plump and tender from the punishing demands of his kisses, before resting his forehead against hers with a sigh. "God, I needed that."

She half laughed, remembering the desperate note of his voice calling her name and hoping that need was all it was. Needing it to be all it was. Defined. Contained. *Manageable.* "Apparently I needed it too."

He cupped her cheek with one hand. "Are you all right?" he said, his voice still choppy. "I didn't give you much of a chance."

She shook her head, looking beyond his shoulder into the now inky night, wondering if she'd only imagined the note of caring in his voice and in his touch? Or was she looking for reasons to find fault now that she'd planted a seed of doubt in her mind?

"I did fine," she said. "Have you eaten?"

"I came straight from my shift."

"Then come inside," she said, ducking under his arm to gather up her scattered clothes, needing space and distance and a cool head to reason. She couldn't think straight when he was naked and this close and he'd just blown her world apart when she'd thought she was the one in control. "I'm sure I can find us something."

His hand caught her upper arm. "Ava? Is something wrong?"

"Nothing's wrong."

"It's just you seem – on edge."

"Do I?" She clutched her crumpled shirt to her chest and forced a smile to her face. She was probably imagining things. Probably just feeling frustrated because her painting wouldn't behave. "Maybe just a bit tired. I'm going to have a shower. Help yourself to a drink."

He picked up her empty wine glass. "Top yours up?"

"Thanks," she said with a nod, and disappeared inside.

CALEB FISHED HIMSELF a beer from the fridge in Ava's self-described "French Provincial meets Rustic" kitchen. He leant against the timber benchtop that had been carved from a fallen tree and definitely had more to do with the latter than the former, even if she'd painted the cupboard doors below it in an antique white, and snapped off the lid, letting the cold liquid slide down his throat. Nothing beat a cold beer after hot sex.

He heard the water turn off in the bathroom and poured a slug of wine into Ava's glass, already anticipating her return. Nothing beat a cold beer after hot sex, that was, unless it was more sex. He'd been right to come. If he'd gone home to his one-bedroom flat, he wouldn't have switched off. He'd probably be on his sixth beer by now, trying to blot out the events of today playing in his head in an endless loop.

But Ava – Ava didn't ask him why or press him for details. Ava didn't complain about his job or pry into his life and his thoughts, searching for details she could turn around and use against him.

She appeared then, wearing her blue robe lashed at her slender waist, shrugging her long hair over her shoulders with her hands in a way that accentuated the golden slice of skin exposed at her chest in the process and, damn, if he didn't feel his cock twitch in appreciation.

"What?" she said, her almond eyes narrowing as her bare feet slapped softly on the terracotta tiled floor as she came towards him.

"You," he said, handing her the glass of wine. "You are a sight for sore eyes."

She took the glass, taking a sip, her eyes above the rim, giving him and his bare chest a quick once over. He'd put on his jeans, even if he hadn't bothered with the button, but that was it.

"You don't look so bad—"

And then she saw it. She came closer, her eyes focusing in on his left shoulder, her fingers lightly tracing over the fancy cursive script across his upper arm.

"Brothers forged in fire," she read. She looked up at him. "When did you get this?"

"The night of my grandfather's memorial service. We all

got one."

Her eyes flicked up again. "All?"

"Well, there were a few of us, including Dylan and two of our firey cousins, Logan and Dare."

He was pretty sure he'd told her he had a twin brother at some point, probably when he'd told her about going to Brisbane for Leonard's memorial service, but other than that, he couldn't ever remember talking about his wider family. And, other than knowing her father was from Singapore and her mother an Australian, he didn't know anything about her family, but that was the kind of relationship they had. When they got together, they didn't waste time talking about family.

"We went drinking after the service, and"—he sucked in a breath—"and, the old man was a real hero. Old school firey with the nous to take firefighting into the current age, without losing the core of what we do." Even if the powers that be were so eager to find a scapegoat for last year's devastating Victorian bushfires, they were willing to crucify him. shook his head at an investigation that seemed to have no good purpose and no end. "So we wanted to honour him somehow, something we could all be part of. A tattoo seemed like a good idea at the time." And it was, although he'd woken up the next day with thunder in his head and a tongue that felt like he'd licked the bottom of a cocky cage and he'd wondered why the hell his arm stung so much. Three weeks on and it was mostly healed. Which meant more than three weeks since he'd seen Ava. Bloody night shift interfering with his sex life. No wonder he'd gone off like a volcano.

She nodded approvingly as she put down her glass and turned towards the fridge door. "Something so permanent should be meaningful."

"Like yours?" he said, placing his hand on the back of her shoulder where he knew the stylized phoenix was inked.

She stiffened under his touch. "Sure," she said lightly – too lightly – agreeing too readily for him to believe he hadn't just hit on a topic she didn't want to discuss.

Warily, he watched her rummaging through the contents of the fridge. Something definitely was bugging her tonight. He knew she liked to keep her feelings to herself, but he'd known her long enough now to know when she was adding another layer of veneer to her shell, and he wasn't convinced he didn't have something to do with her edginess.

She pulled out a container. "How does leftover Mee Goreng sound?"

"Perfect. You know it's my favourite."

He finished off his beer, while she scooped the noodle and prawn dish into bowls and warmed them in the microwave. She had a way of moving he would never tire of. He was no kind of poet, but it occurred even to him that watching her move was like watching silk in motion. Fluid. Graceful. And as elegant as the stylised phoenix on her shoulder. The artist must have been a master to capture the intent in just a few curved lines of ink.

He'd seen plenty of fireys with phoenix tattoos, usually rising from the flames, strong and proud – even Dare had one that just about circled her body – and there the meaning was obvious. But he'd never thought to ask Ava what the tattoo on her shoulder meant to her. He'd figured she'd picked it out from a book of designs because she'd liked it.

Stupid of him, really, but then he hadn't known her beyond the superficial then. Now he knew there was nothing superficial about her at all.

And now he was curious.

"It's a pretty common tatt for fireys to get – a phoenix, I mean," he said, fishing. "You see a lot of them around."

"Oh?" she said, seeming only half interested. "I didn't know."

"A lot of the guys get one after a major fire, like a badge of honour or a public statement that they've come through the worst that life can throw at them."

She nodded. "Like I said, it should be something important. My father forbade me from getting a tattoo, so, of course, I was determined to get one. That was important to me. Can you get the cutlery?"

He dug out cutlery from the drawer and pulled another beer from the fridge while the microwave hummed away, the kitchen filling with the scent of garlic and spices as the machine warmed its contents. Outside the windows, the sky was inky blue, a bright moon turning the trees to dark silhouettes, while inside, his stomach growled appreciatively, and not for the first time he considered himself lucky that he'd come into Ava's orbit. Stunning looking woman, fantastic lover, and exceptional cook. If a man hadn't sworn off marriage for life, he could do a lot worse.

But then, there was so much about her he didn't know. So much she didn't share. She dropped tiny glimpses into her past life like bread crumbs scattered along a path. Once upon a time, he wouldn't have given it a second thought. Now he felt shut out. Excluded. And that was nuts given their relationship was all about the sex, surely?

They sat down opposite each other—the tabletop between them hewn from another slab of the same timber that graced the benchtops—Caleb feeling more unsettled and off-balance than he'd been in a long time, and wondering if today's crash had messed with his head more than he'd realised.

He took a forkful of the warmed up Mee Goreng and flavours exploded on his tongue, and he forgot all about feeling off-balance, and realised how hungry he was. "This is amazing," he said, between mouthfuls.

"It's hot enough?"

And whether she meant warmed up in the microwave enough or chilli hot, it made no difference to his answer. "It's perfect. You know, you're a genius in the kitchen. Not to mention the bedroom for that matter." Then he remembered where they'd just made love. "Outside the bedroom, come to think of it."

The smile in her eyes and her upturned lips put much needed balance back into his off-kilter world. "You know how to make a girl feel good."

He raised his beer in a toast to her. "It's the least I can do. A woman like you deserves to feel good."

AVA WATCHED THE spinning fan above her bed. She wasn't so sure Caleb would think that if he knew exactly what kind of woman she was – and what kind of woman she'd been. What would he think she'd deserve then? To feel good, or to feel the weight of her sordid past around her neck like the slumbering millstone that it was. She closed her eyes, feeling the beast awaken and stir inside her, but unable to block out the thoughts in her head, her mind refusing to rest even as their bodies hummed their way down after another lovemaking session. This time had been nothing like that first, frenetic act. This time had been slow to build and sensual, a pleasurable melding of the carnal with sweet, as they took their time with each other's bodies, took the time to relish every dip and curve of each other, took the time to savour the slide of skin against skin. Even so, when they'd made it to those giddy, teetering heights and she'd come again, it had been with that spellbinding show of light against shadow, and making her wonder, when she was capable of logical thought again, was she really ready to see this end?

No.

She squeezed her eyes more tightly. She liked sex too much. She'd liked the sex almost from the start. Liked the power it had given her over the men who'd visited her bed, even when they thought they were the ones being pleasured.

She liked sex too much to give it up now, on a whim.

A woman like her? Restlessly, she tumbled in his arms again. What would he think a woman like her deserved?

"Aren't you tired?" he asked, as she tried and failed to settle.

"Not really." She was warm in the after sex glow, sure, but her thoughts were cold, like the millstone around her neck.

"Are you thinking about your work?"

"Yes," she answered at length, because there was no way she could tell him what she was really thinking.

"What is it you're working on?" he asked.

"A still life for the exhibition." She shook her head against his shoulder, breathing deep of his underarm scent in the process. Relishing it. There was something about the scent of a strong, clean man. Something honest and raw, and adding another texture to whatever made a man whole. She sighed. "But it's not cooperating."

He kissed her hair. "How so?"

"I don't know." She shrugged her shoulders against him. "There's something unbalanced about it. I worked for hours today, but I just can't see what's wrong with it."

He stroked her arm with his hand. "Is that what's bugging you?"

She looked up at him warily. "Why do you say that?"

"I don't know. It's just this feeling – like something's out of whack. I was worried that—"

"Worried that what?"

"God," he sighed, rubbing his forehead with his free hand. "Nothing. I didn't have a good day. I'm not reading anything particularly well at the moment."

She exhaled then, and pushed herself higher to kiss his stubbled jaw. "Yes, it's the painting. I hate it when it's not working." And that wasn't entirely a lie, because the painting was lodged there too, in that place in her head where she could find questions but no answers.

They lay quietly nestled together, her leg wound over his, his strong arms surrounding her, while her mind continued to tick over. How could she feel so safe, lying here next to Caleb, while at the same time, she felt like she was teetering on the brink of something dangerous? Was the fact it was now getting on for twelve months of shared nights and shared bodies the reason for thinking it must end?

Twelve months of casual hookups, that started in mutual lust and ended in mutual pleasure that sent fireworks spinning through her body and mind.

She couldn't give that up on a whim.

But twelve months – that was beginning to sound permanent…

She sensed the change in him, the slowing of his breathing, the muscles of the arms around her suddenly relaxing. Heavier in sleep. She rested her hand on his chest, felt its even rise and fall, his wiry chest hair tickling her palm, an unfamiliar forest around fingers grown up with hairless Asian skin.

Texture.

The man was a walking canvas.

Her mind drifted to her troubling painting of the blue and white jug and the lemons and the glossy backdrop, the colours reflected in the snowy white yet still not working, and in her mind her random thoughts merged and coalesced and like a bolt the answer hit her.

Of course! Carefully, she eased out from under his arms. He stirred but didn't waken as she slipped from the bed and into her artist shirt and padded barefoot to her studio. She snapped on the lights and night turned into day. In the centre of the room stood her easel bearing her problematic canvas while adjacent sat an old leather chesterfield where she flopped when she was too tired to make it to bed. Canvases lined the two walls, mostly finished in readiness for her upcoming exhibition, the wall of windows overlooking the valley made up the third and the fourth comprised shelving filled with paints and art books and boxes and boxes of stuff that she'd kept because it might be useful some day – and in one of them…

It was in an old vintage cardboard suitcase that she found

it, folded into a square and tucked away because one day she might need it. She'd found it in a fabric shop in a box of remnants and, while it had been the shifting colour of the piece that had caught her eye, it was the compulsion to reach out and touch the piece of fabric that had sealed the deal.

Reverently she unfolded it, feeling a frisson of excitement as the midnight blue fabric sprang to life in the light. How had she forgotten it until now? She palmed her hand against the short dense pile, put it to her cheek and felt its velvet touch and felt that same excitement she'd had the day she'd found it.

Texture.

She looked at the canvas she'd been struggling with, of her favourite jug filled with a posy of plump yellow lemons from a neighbour's garden and it was so blindingly obvious now why it was never going to work against a stark white background.

It took the best part of half an hour reworking the still life, positioning the fabric just right, so just like the hills and valleys around her, the light shone or was swallowed up in the shadowy depths. Until finally she was happy and she picked up her paintbrush and got to work.

Chapter Three

CALEB'S PHONE WOKE him in the predawn grey. He blinked into wakefulness as he groped for it, suddenly aware of the cool of the sheets beside him and the absence of Ava. Painting, he figured she'd be, up with the dawn no doubt, as she often seemed to be on the occasional nights he stayed over.

He rubbed his eyes as he checked the screen, saw it was his station officer calling, and picked up. "Mike? What's happening?"

"The baby," he said, and Caleb's stomach clenched because straight away he knew what baby he was calling about. "We've just got word from the hospital, it's a boy and he's doing well."

Caleb put a hand to his head as he let go a breath he hadn't realised he'd been holding. "That's good." At least they'd managed to salvage something from the tragedy that had been yesterday. "Real good."

"And mate, get this. The father wants to meet you."

"What?"

"He heard what happened. He reckons if you hadn't been there wrangling those Jaws of Life in time, he'd be looking at buying two coffins right now, instead of one. He wants to thank you personally. Not yet, the baby's still in hospital and the father wants to get over the funeral and everything, but he said he'd call when he's ready."

Caleb closed his eyes and thought about a baby who'd never know his mother and a man who'd lost his wife yesterday, and who wanted to thank the man who, in spite of his best efforts, had watched the wife die and hadn't been able to do a damn thing to prevent it.

Christ. What a job. Because, while he knew he'd done everything possible to extract the woman from the wreckage in the fastest possible time and the best possible result, he also knew he'd be forever plagued with thoughts that things might have ended up better if he'd done things differently.

"Caleb? You there?"

His voice, when it came, was thick with the tangle of emotions. "I'm here."

"Good. Only I see you're down to volunteer on the barbeque at the CFS stall at the Ashton Show next weekend? You still good for a couple of hours in the morning taking care of the sausage sizzle?"

"You wouldn't be trying to change the subject, would you?"

There was a moment's hesitation, before, "Well, yeah. Maybe."

And Caleb snorted and thanked Christ for mates who knew what it was like to be on the receiving end of news like Mike had just delivered, bittersweet news that reminded them all over again about the tragedy of the day before, and how to give them something else to think about.

He put down his mobile and lay back in bed for a minute, listening to the chorus of birdsong in the surrounding bush, the magpies and parrots and kookaburras all trying to outdo each other in their enthusiasm to greet the new day.

So it was almost time for the local hills show again? Ava would be there too, painting kids' faces to raise funds for charity, like she'd been doing the first time they'd met. Heck, was it a year ago already? Bloody hell, that had gone quickly. He'd bet neither one of them had thought they'd still be seeing each other after this long.

He had Richo to thank for meeting Ava, not that he was going to about to tell him any time soon, because then he'd have to tell him about Ava, and Richo would bang on about it when there was really nothing to tell. But it had been Richo who'd volunteered to help out the CFS stand at the show a couple of years back, and then last year he'd roped Caleb in to help with the sausage sizzle, to give the local CFS guys a chance to spray a few hoses and give the local kids a ride around the footy oval on their appliances.

Local kids with faces painted, so they looked like butterflies or spidermen or cats or dogs. Faces painted by Ava. And, in a lull in the traffic, he and his mates on the barbeque had drawn straws to see who should get his face painted to drum up business. He'd drawn the short straw, and his colleagues had happily sent him off, but as it had turned out, he'd won the best prize of all, because he'd sat there with his eyes closed and every stroke of her brush had been a direct hit to his groin.

By the end of it, he'd been nursing a hard-on so debilitating, he'd had to stay sitting down and making small talk about the weather for fifteen minutes while she painted the next kid's face.

Butterflies, he'd had to tell himself, think about butterflies or fairies, pixies or kittens. Told himself to forget about the whisper soft yet carnal stroke of her brush on his skin.

And afterwards, when she was packing up her table and chairs and paints in the back of her small hatchback, he'd dropped over and asked for her number, and she'd told him she wasn't looking for a relationship. "Neither am I," he'd said. "So how about we settle for sex?"

She'd cocked her head and asked him if he was always this direct, and he'd realised, hell no. Which was probably what had got him stuck in his go-nowhere marriage for long after its use by date, and why he was doing things differently from now on. Forget happy ever after, he'd figured. He'd settle for happy every now and then.

And so far, it was proving to be the right decision.

Somewhere across the valley, an old man koala was grunting up a storm, advertising his machismo. Damn straight, Caleb thought, looking at the sheet tenting over his own equipment. He only had to think about Ava to get a hard-on. He pulled on his jeans to go find her.

The dark layers of the sky were peeling back to shades of pink and blue, the air crisp and cool outside. He sniffed at the air, instinctively testing for smoke and finding none, but Ava he found right where he suspected he would. She was in the studio feverishly working, her painter's shirt tail barely covering her naked ass, her golden skinned legs long and bare below, and swaying evocatively this way and that as she worked. He didn't interrupt her. He knew better than that, at least before he came bearing a pot of coffee.

Ten minutes later he was back. Her movements were slower now, her brush adding tiny detail after detail, before she took a step back, looked at her still life arrangement and the canvas on the easel, and put down her brush.

"Good morning," he said. "How's it going?"

She spun around, the golden highlights in her eyes almost luminescent, her whole face lit up. "I think I got it!" she said. "It was flat before, and lifeless, but then I worked out what was wrong."

He moved closer to study the painting behind her, the jug and the brightly coloured lemons against a rich velvet backdrop that rippled with light and looked for all the world that if you just reached out a finger, you would feel the softness of its pile.

"How do you do that?" he asked, feeling genuine awe

and wonder. "How do you turn a two-dimensional canvas into something that looks so realistic?"

She shrugged. "It takes time, but I'd done the painstaking work earlier – it was the background I realised wasn't working." She rubbed her hands together as she surveyed her canvas once more. "You made me realise what was missing."

"Me?"

She turned back to him and damned if there wasn't something wicked in her smile. "To be more precise, it was the smell of your underarms and the curl of your chest hair around my fingers that made me see it."

He looked down at his chest, took a mock sniff under one arm. "What?"

She shook her head, still smiling, "Don't ask," she said, as she curled herself catlike down on the old leather chesterfield, her legs tucked beneath her, the shirt rising at the sides to expose the glorious curve of her naked hip. God, could she do nothing that didn't make him think of silk and sex? "Just pour me that coffee."

He did just that, saying, "I swear I will never understand women."

"You're not supposed to. That would take all the fun out of it."

He handed her the cup of the steaming brew and she put it to her nose and inhaled deeply, taking the tiniest of sips before resting it down on the table alongside to cool.

"How long have you been working?" he asked, as he

poured himself a mug and went back to study the painting, one hand on his hip, the other nursing his mug.

"Since you fell asleep," she said from the sofa behind him.

"You've been at this all night?"

"I had to, once I figured it out. I'll sleep later. I'm too happy to sleep now."

"You should be. It's brilliant." He tilted his head to the side and brought his coffee to his mouth.

"Hang on," she said suddenly. "Don't move."

He half turned, hearing her scrabbling around behind him. "What?"

"No. Go back the way you were. Hand on hip, looking at the picture. That's it."

"Ava?"

"This won't take a moment. Just stay like that, okay?"

He heard soft noises behind him, the swipe of pencil and the rub of her thumb against the page and he stiffened, feeling a little like he was under a microscope. "What are you doing?" Ava had never used him as one of her models and it was strangely unsettling.

"Doing what I do. Capturing something of beauty."

He snorted at that. "Yeah, right." But still his skin tingled all over with every skating stroke of her pencil. He knew he was in good shape physically. Keeping fit was part and parcel of the job and it was never a hassle to get on one of his bikes and ride or work out at home or in the station gym. It was something else entirely to be told he was a "thing of beauty."

"So is this how it feels to be objectified?" he asked, half joking.

"You tell me. But speaking of objects…'

He heard the slap of her sketchbook against the leather of the lounge, heard the roll of her pencil across the page and the soft plop as it landed on the sofa.

"Are we done?" he asked, wondering if he was ever going to get to drink this damn cup of coffee.

"Not quite. Stay there. Just a minute longer."

He took a breath and waited. "Now what are you doing?"

The brush of her bare nipples against his back and her slim fingers circling low on his waist told him all he needed to know, even if he did nearly drop the mug in the process. "Oh."

She pressed a kiss to his shoulder blade and he felt the smile on her lips and the smooth curve of her belly against his butt. "Can I move yet?"

"No rush," she said, her nimble fingers working at his zipper, sliding it all the way down while her nipples kept making lazy circles on his back that set his flesh on fire. "I like you like this."

He swallowed, feeling the kick in his pants before her hands even found him. "Someone's in a good mood today." His voice had suddenly gone down an octave, but then, why should his blood be the only thing headed in that direction?

"I am," she purred, raining kisses over his skin. "I'm sorry. I didn't realise how frustrated I was yesterday."

"You're not feeling frustrated now?"

"No, not at all."

At least that made one of them. She released his hardening dick from his pants and squeezed her hands around it and he groaned. "Ava," he warned.

But she was already on the move, liquid silk weaving around his body. She slid one hand around his, leading his mug to her mouth and taking a sip of his coffee, before kissing him on his lips bringing coffee and heat and the warm, sensual taste of Ava swirling in his mouth.

He reached for her then, and she brushed his hand away.

"No." She took the mug, placing it on the bench alongside, and looked up at him, her cognac eyes flickering with wicked intent. before dropping to her knees before him, her seeking hands already encircling their target and introducing it to her mouth.

Oh. My. God!

"I want to thank you," she said, as she watched his face while her lips danced like satin against his straining tip, the slick heat of her mouth and her warm breath combining into a delicious tease, "for helping me work it out."

"My pleasure," he croaked through a throat two sizes too small, although he really didn't have a clue what he'd done to deserve it.

And it was. His pleasure. Every bit of it. Every hot flick of her tongue, every sizzling wrap of her lips around his cock. Every deep suck of her hot mouth. And he had every good intention of being a considerate lover and choosing when the time was right to flip her over and pleasure her likewise before burying himself deep inside her, when she surprised him by skidding her hands down low and squeezing her fingers into the tight bunches of his butt, her fingernails spiking into his crease, there was nothing else to do but tangle his hands in her hair and hang on for dear life.

Though, as it turned out, hanging on wasn't an option. Not for long.

He erupted in a blinding flash of wildfire that consumed his mind and his thoughts and left nothing but the strangest feeling that nothing in his world had ever been so right.

CALEB MADE A second pot of coffee to replace the one that had gone cold, while Ava slipped on her shirt and picked up where she'd left with her sketch book on the chesterfield. "Can I see?" he asked, when he got back.

"Sure." She turned the book towards him and there he was, or at least his back, shaded in charcoal, from his neck bunching of muscle at his shoulder to the shaded curve of his spine and the loose wrap of denim at his hips. "Wow."

"I know. It's good. I think I've worked out my next few works for my exhibition."

"You have?" He wasn't sure he wanted to hear this.

"This is what I needed." She waved her arm around the canvases lining the wall. "These are good, but I knew I needed something more, something to take it to the next level, and this"—she held up the sketchbook—"this will give the collection more depth and give me more chance of picking up commission work. Plus, I bet they'll sell like hotcakes too."

He snorted. "You mean beefcakes."

"I'm serious. You have a beautiful body, Caleb. It's a work of art. Why shouldn't it be immortalized on paper and admired?"

"Look Ava," he said, lifting up her feet so he could park himself alongside her on the sofa before pulling them over his lap "Is that such a good idea? I thought you wanted to keep this thing private. If you go slapping up a whole heap of pictures of me on a wall wearing not a hell of a lot, somebody's going to twig."

"Nobody will know it's you. I'll just do torsos, no heads. You'll be identified only as 'Male Nude' numbers one, two, three and four. Okay?"

"You want to do four of these? Seriously?"

"One's not enough. I'm seeing these on an end wall. And they won't be all the same. There's just something about the way your body moves. I'll know what I want to draw when I see it."

"But no heads?"

She crossed her heart with a finger. "I swear."
"And no anything elses, for that matter."
She smiled. "It's a deal."

Chapter Four

CALEB WAS WHISTLING when he clocked on for his shift the next day. He spent forty-five minutes in the gym sweating his way through crunches and planks and push-ups before he hit the weights room and set to enough repetitions to lift his own bodyweight ten times over. He was still whistling when he hit the showers. God, he felt better than when he'd walked out of the station thirty-six hours ago, but spending time with Ava could do that. She didn't ask for anything. She didn't take anything he didn't want to give. And what she gave him was pure gold.

She'd sketched him again too – made him stop when he was getting dressed to leave and pulling his shirt over his shoulders – and he'd had to stay there immobile for five minutes while his skin tingled and her pencil worked over-time on the page.

Him, a life model. Who knew? He snorted with the sheer improbability of it.

Richo was tying up his boots as Caleb uniformed up. "Somebody's sure in a good mood today."

"Why wouldn't I be? It's a beautiful day."

His mate glanced out the window unconvinced. "Nope, that doesn't cut it. If a man didn't know better, he'd say someone was getting laid."

Caleb slapped his crew mate on the back. Richo was known about the station as a lady's man. At least, that was what he liked to tell anyone who cared to listen. There wasn't a woman in the station that hadn't been propositioned. Probably in the entire force.

"What's the problem, Richo? You not getting any?"

Richo puffed up his chest. "Hey, I get plenty."

And Caleb just laughed as the incident bell sounded and said, "Congratulations."

"What have we got?" Tina, another crew mate asked a scant minute later, as the crew piled into the truck. He could read the faces of his crew and knew they were already on full alert, primed for action and whatever the day could throw at them.

"Something a bit different," he told them as the truck pulled out of the station, not bothering with the siren. "We've got a woman who's apparently got a bunch of birds nesting in her chimney."

"What the fuck?" said Richo, looking sideways at the others.

"Could be worse," Tina said with a laugh. "Could be bats in the belfry."

Richo snorted. "Sure *she* hasn't got bats in the belfry?"

Caleb listened to the banter between his crew mates. This was a new one on him too, but that was okay. They were always being called upon to rescue animals and wildlife in odd circumstances and they were always happy to help if they weren't already busy attending a major incident. Just the other week they'd had to use the Bronto Skylift to reach an injured koala with a joey that had been hit by a car crossing a road. The joey had been found crying on the side of the road and fauna rescue notified, but by the time they'd arrived, the bleeding mother had managed to clamber her way up to the top reaches of a nearby gum tree.

Caleb had accompanied the wildlife experts in the cage of the Bronto to reach the frightened animal and force it down the tree to the ground where it was scooped into a cage and reunited with its baby, before being whisked off to a local vet for attention to what turned out to be, thankfully, minor wounds needing only a few stitches.

Yeah, incidents like this made for a pleasant change.

They pulled up outside an elegant old Queen Anne villa set high in the foothills amongst what must have been two acres of orchard and gardens. A "for sale" sign out the front brandished a big "sold" sticker.

"Bloody hell," Richo said as they walked down the driveway towards the house. "Check out the turret."

Tina snorted. "You've got a one track mind, Richo."

Caleb appreciated the joke even as he was busy taking in the house. Not only the turret and the crenelated entry porch with a grand arch below, but the chimneys. Big ones. They sure didn't build them like that anymore.

"Thank heavens you're here," said a sixty-something woman bursting out of the front door to greet them. "I didn't know who else to call."

She introduced herself as Eleanor and led them into the sprawling house, talking nineteen to the dozen as she wove her way through expansive rooms shrunken by the old, overstuffed furniture and stack of packing boxes in various stages of being filled. "It started just before the auction, you see. First a fluttering sound, and then squeaking. At first I was afraid they were rats. Imagine that, rats, just when you're trying to sell your house! So I called a chimney sweep but they said they don't deal with live animals in chimneys and I had to call a pest exterminator. And I called a pest exterminator but they asked if I was sure they were rats and by that stage I wasn't because their squeaking sounded more like cheeping and maybe they could be parrots. At least, they sound more like parrots now than rats. We've got fruit trees outside and the parrots are always into the fruit and so it could be. And so I called Fauna Rescue, because if they're parrots, they're protected, you see, and they'll take the chicks and care for them, but they needed to be old enough to survive the trauma and they needed someone to get them out because they don't have the equipment and how on earth are they supposed to get out otherwise? Learn to fly straight up a chimney?" She stopped in front of a massive open fireplace topped by an equally massive mantelpiece bearing a mirror that went all the way to the ceiling which had to be twelve-foot high if it was an inch, thought Caleb, and then there would be a few feet of the chimney through the roof above. How indeed could they fly out of there? It would be nothing like falling out of a tree.

"But if you can get them out," Eleanor continued, "I've got the name and address of a local carer who'll take them and I've promised to deliver them. If you can get them out, that is."

Caleb nodded. At least she'd got that angle covered. Now all he had to do was work out how to get them out. "And the birds are somewhere inside this lot?

"I think they're somewhere behind here," the woman said, pointing to the timber frame below the mantelpiece, "just behind this. There's a baffle over the fireplace, and it's closed when it's not in use, and I think they must be nesting there, but I tried to move the handle and it seems to be jammed shut. You can hear them, especially at meal times. They're so loud then. When they go quiet, I worry they might have died. But it would be terrible if they died in there wouldn't it? Imagine the smell! But they could die if anything happened to the parents and they didn't come back. Anything could happen. And the new owners move in next week, and I just didn't know what to do and I'm just so glad you're here."

And four firies in yellow uniforms blinked at each other

and lined up along the wide fireplace, which had been brooding silently by while the owner voiced every one of her fears in almost the same sentence, and put their ears to the wood, and listened and heard…

Absolutely nothing.

Richo looked at Caleb, his eyes ducking horizontal towards the anxious woman standing nearby, before he winked and mouthed "bats' and Caleb curled his hand into a fist and slammed the side of it into the wood, and somewhere inside all hell broke loose and there was cheeping and fluttering and mad swooping sounds.

"You see," said the woman triumphantly. "I'm not imagining it, am I? There's definitely something in there."

"Something sure is," Caleb said, instructing Richo to grab some tarpaulins from the truck to lay on the carpet. He wasn't the most junior in the crew – Matt was the rookie – but Richo deserved to be made to fetch and carry after the crack about the woman. She might be able to talk nonstop for ten minutes without drawing breath, but she wasn't imagining anything. "Now we just have to work out how to get whatever it is out."

Tina radioed back to base to let them know what they were faced with while they lay the tarpaulins down in front of the fire place in preparation for opening the baffle, which just as the woman said, was stuck fast when Caleb tested it, with bits raining down and what sounded like something tap dancing on the top.

"Do you think the birds have jammed it with their nest?" the woman asked.

Caleb suspected it was probably jammed up with bird poo, but he didn't want to say so. "If it's parrots, there shouldn't be a nest," he said. "They usually nest in hollow tree trunks and the like, just using whatever space is available. Here," he said to Richo, "help us out with a bit of grunt, and see if we can't move this thing."

They combined their efforts and gave the lever an almighty shove and finally they budged it a fraction, and then a fraction more until it ground open with a rush, bringing down a cloud of debris and soot until the air in the room was cloudy and filled with the pungent scent of birds.

Richo coughed and flicked a few bits of dried bird poo from his hair and tiny feather from his eyebrow. "That's foul!"

Caleb smiled – he'd managed to duck the worst of it – and had Tina pass him a torch. "Nope. They'd be chickens in that case."

"Ha, bloody ha," said his mate, still swiping at the flecks on his uniform.

"So where are the birds?" said Tina, squatting down and looking up the dusty chimney to follow the beam of Caleb's torchlight. "I can still hear them."

"They're playing hard to get." He turned to their hostess. "Eleanor, have you got a box or something?"

"Would a packing box do?"

"Perfect," he said. "Hand it to Sooty over here. Richo, you stand by for incoming. And just be ready to cover the top."

And Caleb grabbed hold of the mantelpiece with one hand and leaned low under the fireplace and reached up with his other, searching the top of the now open baffle lid. Funny, he thought, because in all his years of training and all his scores animal and wildlife rescues, he'd never once come across anything like this. But he'd grown up just up the hill at Reynolds Ridge where the parrots lived in the hollows of trees and drove the orchardists crazy in cherry season, and he must have learned something useful along the way.

He shook his head though, at the crazy bloody birds that chose a chimney to nest in. Safer than a tree hollow where a passing kookaburra might hear the chicks and fancy a light meal perhaps, but god only knew how the parents thought their chicks were going to learn to fly. He'd heard of the expression, helicopter parents, but this was ridiculous.

He skated his gloved hand along the metal roof. Little buggers were in here somewhere. He'd caught a glimpse of them darting away from the beam of light, trying to hide in the shadows.

Finally, he got his hand around flailing creature and brought it out and down. About six to eight inches long with soot disguising its bright plumage, the nestling wasn't giving in easy, squawking a mighty protest. Richo held the box lid open and Caleb pushed in the unhappy bird to a flurry of feathers and shrieks.

"Oh my," Eleanor said, "you got it. Well done."

"There's more," Caleb said, already going back under the mantel. He had a feel for the terrain this time and he managed to scoop the second one up even faster. The third proved trickier just because it had more space to run around to try to evade capture, but finally that one was safe in his gloved hand too. He did a final sweep with his hand and the torchlight but couldn't find any more.

The birds didn't seem all that happy at being reunited in the box, screeching and banging and flapping their wings, so that Richo had a job to keep the lid from surging open, the birds surprisingly strong despite their immaturity.

"That's it," said Caleb, rubbing his gloves together, shouting to make himself heard over the cacophony of shrieks and bangs coming from the box. "You might want to cover the box with a blanket so it's darker and they think they're back in the chimney and settle again."

And Eleanor nodded up at him over the squawking box and he saw a cheeky glimmer in her eyes. "You really think they'll settle?"

He couldn't help but smile, even as he shrugged and folded up a tarp. "It's worth a shot."

They were on their way back to the station, the completion of the incident radioed in, when Richo chortled to himself.

"What?" said Caleb.

"My mum always used to complain when the five of us kids piled into the back of the car after school. Said it sounded like a box of birds." He grinned. "Poor Mum, now I know what she meant."

THE REST OF the week passed, happily, just as uneventfully for Caleb. He was looking forward to Sunday and working at the Ashton Show and seeing Ava again. And then he remembered the feel of her clever tongue swirling around his dick, and he was looking forward to a whole lot more besides. There were times he kind of wished he hadn't agreed to this arrangement, where they lived and worked separate lives and came together only occasionally to burn up the sheets – thinking how good would it be to go home to Ava every night, and have her and her hot body on tap. But that wasn't how their arrangement worked. Sex was what he'd offered and she'd accepted. Neither of them had been looking for a relationship and he'd been happy to agree with her terms if it meant having the best sex of his life.

Besides, after Angie, he could see how quickly the little happy ever fantasy could turn south. Nope, he thought with a sigh, remembering the grief and pain that had been those torrid years, better to have a taste of paradise every now and then, than risk paradise turning into hell on earth.

Even if it didn't stop him thinking about it.

But he'd see her Sunday, and meanwhile, there was plen-

ty to do at the station to keep him busy. There was a foun-
tain on a main street due to a burst water main, and he'd
spent a morning in wet weather gear directing vehicles
around while the water department battled to turn off the
supply. There'd been a primary school visit, where they'd
turned on the flashing lights and the siren to give the kids a
thrill and show how cool it was to be a firefighter while
educating kids to call triple zero in an emergency in the
process. And then there were days where the entire crew
spent time checking and polishing every single thing that
moved or not on their appliances.

This was the flipside of the hard-core recovery work, and,
while Caleb loved the adrenaline rush of getting in and
getting dirty, there was a lot to be said for tackling the day-
to-day nitty-gritty of station work so that when the going got
tough, the equipment didn't let them down.

And, meantime, everyone it seemed kept an eye on the
weather forecast. They'd been blessed with a good spring
season, with good rainfall, but with that had come high
growth in the understory. And summer was proving unchar-
acteristically gentle so far. December had morphed into
January with the occasional burst of heat, but thankfully
with none of the heatwaves that rolled on with temperatures
well over the old century for days and nights. It was when
the temperatures soared and that hot north wind came down
from the baking dry interior of Australia that put the wind
up everyone, and had every nostril twitching. A fire in the

Adelaide Hills in those circumstances was damn near unstoppable.

The forecast for the Ashton Show looked okay for now, but there was hot weather following, he could see on the forecast, a slow-moving high predicted to lob over the red desert centre of Australia and stay there, directing hot northerly winds straight down towards them.

Nobody was looking forward to that.

CALEB WAS IN his spare room doing bench presses the day before the show when Ava surprised him by calling. "Are you free tonight? I want to show you something. I'll be in the studio." There was excitement in her voice that was contagious and Caleb found himself at her house inside twenty minutes.

As his feet crunched down the gravel path from the car, his eyes couldn't help but be drawn to the spectacular view Ava had over the Uriarra Gorge, with its steep cliffs and treed valleys and ridgetops – terrain both beautiful and hard to protect in a bushfire situation – and he made a mental note to check Ava's rooftop sprinkler system given the upcoming weather forecast.

He understood people wanted to live in the Adelaide Hills. Hell, he'd grown up hereabouts himself with his brother, with an entire range of hills and valleys for their back yard. Together they'd roamed far and wide, terrorizing the local wildlife, by sending mobs of grazing kangaroos scattering as they'd chased them out of grasslands, and climbing trees trying to reach the koalas nestled high in the branches, only to have them climb even further out of range. In turn they'd been terrorized when they'd stumbled upon the odd snake basking in the sunshine on the path in front of them.

While in winter they'd played alongside the rushing creeks and waterfalls of the valleys and gorges, chasing frogs and sending pieces of bark scudding down the rapid waters.

It had been the best kind of childhood and he knew better than anyone how special it was to live up this way. But he'd seen the fires too, that had ravaged the hills from time to time, that scorched the earth and left nothing in their wake, and were an ever present danger to life and property each and every summer, and one look at where Ava lived and a proper bushfire sprinkler system had been the first thing he'd suggested she get installed. That and a retreat room behind the studio where the studio backed into the earth wall of the slight rise behind, in case things got too rough and there was no way out. And, to her credit, she'd seen the sense in that and agreed. He'd put in the sprinklers and diesel pump and he'd lined the retreat room with concrete panelling to insulate it. Small things, but worthwhile, especially for a woman on her own.

He'd checked the diesel pump was working okay before the beginning of summer, and made sure she checked it weekly, but it was high time he checked it again.

There was music coming from the studio and Caleb recognised it as Ava's favourite playlist. He didn't know the names of any of the singers – his music tastes had stalled sometime around the Red Hot Chili Peppers – but that just added to the mystery and the exoticism that was Ava. God only knew how he'd ever got the courage to approach her.

She was working on a canvas when he rapped on the glass. She looked up and smiled and it was a good thing he wasn't flammable because one hundred watts zapped its way straight to his groin. She met him half way across the room, taking his head in her hands, the kiss she gave him fast and furious and full of promise, and when she put his head away, her cognac eyes were damned near glowing.

"Come and see," she said, taking his hand and leading him to the easel.

"It's the first one, remember? When you were looking at the still life."

He blinked. He remembered. But he also remembered it was the size of a page in a book. This was at least two feet high. "What happened to the other one? The small one?"

"That was just a sketch." She laced her fingers in his. "Well? What do you think?"

What could he say? He'd thought the sketch was the real deal, but now he looked at the likeness of his back, his muscles rendered in myriad shades of charcoal and oil pastels that seemed to capture the very texture of his skin in the skilful use of light and shade. And there, on the back of his arm, the last three letters of his tattoo.

He frowned as he pointed it out. "I thought you said nobody would know it was me."

"How could anyone recognise you from that?"

"My brother might."

"Is he in the market for artworks and likely to be at the exhibition?"

"Well, no." There was that. "But—"

"I've got a couple of ideas for others," she said, discounting his protest without waiting to hear it.

"I thought you said you'd know it when you saw it."

"I know. But the exhibition's in less than a month, and I need to get busy. And if they don't work, we'll try something else." Her lips curved into a smile. "So I was thinking…'

Which was how Caleb found himself naked in Ava's shower not ten minutes later, hands behind his neck with water cascading down over his upturned face and down his chest and abdomen, while Ava sat on the lid of the toilet seat and scribbled feverishly in her sketchbook. She was drawing his torso, he knew, and drawing the line at chin and hips, but for the life of him he couldn't rid himself this feeling of being watched, and it showed.

"Do other life models have this problem?" he asked, his cock swelling with every passing minute.

"Quit complaining," she simply said.

"It's hardly fair," he said into the stream of water. "I'm

standing under here naked and you're fully dressed.

"Is that what you're bitching about? If you promise not to move, I can fix that."

"What did you say?" he spluttered.

"Don't move!"

So he stayed right where he was with the water pouring over his head but somehow the knowledge she'd got herself buck naked too didn't help with his problem one little bit. He didn't have to open his eyes to know exactly how she'd look sitting there without a stitch on, with her slim shoulders and her slender waist flaring to her hips, and her breasts peaked with those gorgeous dark nipples he was a major fan of.

He groaned. "It's not helping!" If this wasn't water torture, he didn't know what was.

"It's okay. I'm done."

"Thank god. So what have you got planned next," he asked, snapping off the taps and reaching for a towel.

And she rose from the side of bath to meet him wearing a smile and nothing more. "Me."

Chapter Five

THEY MADE LOVE on her big bed watching the sun go down outside her big picture windows and then she sketched him lying on his stomach, his arms splayed, on the unmade sheets while the sunlight streamed through the window, making his skin glow.

"I'm going for a look of utter abandonment here," she told him, her pencil flying in strokes over the page.

From the pillows where his head was buried came a muffled groan. "I think I've found it."

She smiled. He had good reason to look spent. They both did. But she'd got to feeling sexy as hell watching Caleb in that shower with the water running in streamlets over him, so what was a girl supposed to do but ravage him?

And she owed him. She couldn't remember a time when she'd enjoyed her work more. Maybe it was because that last still life had been so problematic, but it was refreshing to be working on something completely different. And now, given Caleb's cooperation, she'd have the thirty artworks she'd agreed to supply for her upcoming exhibition without having to resort to including any she wasn't quite in love with herself, the ones that didn't quite make the grade for whatever reason.

Because she had no doubts about this series though, as his beautiful body took form on the page. These were definitely going to make the grade. Maybe it was something she should do more of. It was such a pleasure to be working with the human form again, something she hadn't done for too long.

The buzz of her phone interrupted her. "Hang on," she told him, conscious of the setting sun and wanting to finish her sketch while she still had the light. "I'll be right back." There were only a handful of people who had her number and even less who had cause to call tonight and she'd already decided before she picked up that it must be the Evan from EJ's Gallery wanting a progress report from her before actively promoting the upcoming exhibition. There were times she almost wished she had someone who could handle all the administration and marketing of her career so she could fully concentrate on her art, but then she remembered Rene and his lies and the bitter disappointment of learning yet another person had betrayed her and she wasn't prepared to go there again. Besides. The way the collection was coming together, this was one call she wouldn't mind taking. It would only take a moment.

"Evan," she said, picking up.

Except it wasn't him.

And as she listened, just like the fading colour in the sky, all the light and colour in her life leached away, until she sat down trembling in the half-light, her hand still cradling her phone, traitor to the dark world she'd never quite left behind.

"Ava?"

She blinked, sucking in air, not knowing how long she'd been sitting here in the gathering gloom. "I'm here," she said, although her voice even to her sounded a long way away.

"What's wrong?" he said, kneeling down on his haunches alongside her. "Who was that?"

She stared blindly ahead of her through scratchy eyes, although there were no tears. She'd always known there would be no tears when it happened. It was half her life ago and she'd shed all the tears she was ever going to shed, until there was nothing left behind but a cold, hard anger. Although she'd never expected to feel so – *blindsided*.

"It was someone from a law firm in Singapore. I didn't catch his name." She didn't even know how they had her number. How the hell did they get her number?

"What did they want?"

"It's my parents." She turned her head towards him, saw the concern in his eyes, and had to turn away. "There was a car crash. They're dead."

"Oh, Ava." He put his arms around her, and yet all she could feel was the oppressive hand of her father lifting, knowing he could never hurt her again. That, and a dank blanket of remembrance.

"It's okay," she said, shrugging out of his embrace, wishing she could shrug off the memories as easily. "Really, it's okay." She looked out the window, saw the day had turned to twilight. "Damn," she said, rising from the chair. "We lost the light."

"Ava?"

"I'm sorry, Caleb. I'll just have to try to finish from what I've got." She attempted a smile as she headed for the fridge. "I'm sure I won't have any trouble remembering how you look naked. Are you hungry? I can make us up something."

Caleb sprang up beside her and the next moment the lights in the kitchen burst on, transforming dusk into daylight. She winced at the stark bright of the lights, and then he was by her side. He was wearing just a towel slung low on his hips. How hadn't she noticed that little detail before? So unlike her.

"Why are you worried about eating? For god's sake, Ava, you just lost your parents."

"Yes, I know. I thought it was Evan Jones – the gallery owner – checking up to see how the collection was going." She gave a little half laugh. "I sure got that wrong. Oh well, are you sure you don't want something to eat?"

Beside her, Caleb ran one hand through his hair and sighed. "Listen, Ava, I know this must be hard for you, being so far away and all."

"What baffles me is how they got my number."

"What?"

"I never gave it to anyone, let alone my father's solicitors. So how did they get it?"

"Is that the most important thing to be worrying about right now?"

She pulled open the fridge door and stared blankly at the shelves. She'd always known it wouldn't take much to track down her new name if they'd wanted to – she was an artist with a website and who'd featured in at least a dozen newspaper and online articles – she wasn't exactly invisible. But her private phone number? "Why would they even want it?" Unless it was so her father could reach out, even in death, to let her know that she'd never really escaped. That he was still in control.

She shivered. *Never again.*

"You've had a shock," said the man beside her. "I felt like the ground had pulled from beneath my feet when I heard my grandfather had died, even though Leonard was a much older man. It's the finality of death. There's no going back."

She blinked over at him. It was like he was having a conversation about something else or why would he even say such a thing? Why would he imagine that she'd want to go back?

She pulled a bottle from inside the fridge door. "I think I need a drink."

He found her a glass and she gave thanks as she poured

herself a sizeable slug. At least he hadn't tried to talk her out of that. She made to put the bottle back in the fridge and thought better of it, picking up both glass and bottle and heading for the sofa.

She took a gulp of her wine, only half aware of the sound of Caleb moving around behind her. How long had her father known where she was? Had he had his cronies watching her all this time? What else did they know?

And all this time, she'd imagined she was free. Out of sight. Out of reach. Safe.

Bastards.

Even in death they wouldn't let her go.

Caleb put a beer down on the coffee table and set himself down beside her, swivelled sideways, his arm along the sofa at her back. He reached his other hand over and squeezed her. "I'm sorry, Ava, it's rough. I know."

And suddenly his assumption that he knew something of what she was feeling was too much.

She pulled her hand free. "What makes you think you know anything of what I'm feeling?" It might be rough news, difficult, even problematic, but he knew nothing of the why. He knew nothing of why she might in fact be happy her parents were dead.

At last.

She took another gulp of her wine too fast, the cold liquid splashing on her cheek. She swiped at it with the back of her hand while she worked out whether it was even worth trying to explain, and promptly decided it wasn't.

She didn't owe anyone an explanation. "Look, Caleb, I'm sorry our evening got cut short, but, right now, I think it's better that you go."

"I'm not going anywhere, not while you're like this."

She tossed up her chin. "What am I like?"

"I don't know. Hurting. Angry. Grieving. Confused. Probably all of the above. It's normal. It's the shock."

She snorted, because of course the news of the loss of a parent or even two must be accompanied by earth shattering grief. But she would admit to the anger. She was angry that her father had lived so many years when she had wished him dead. She was angry that her mother had as good as fed her to the lions. "You don't know the first thing about how I feel. *Now*, will you go?"

"Is that what you really want?"

"Do I really need to say it again?"

He sighed, like she was a problem child who was refusing to eat her vegetables rather than a grown woman who knew her own feelings and what she needed, but he got up from the sofa.

"All right, I'll go. But I want you to know, you don't have to face this all yourself. When's the funeral? I've got leave owing. I'll come with you."

"You'll what?" She snorted. "What on earth are you talking about?"

"I'm assuming it's going to be held in Singapore, so I'll

come too. And not as a lover. But as a friend, to support you."

She shook her head, not making sense of any of it. "Why would you even suggest that? I didn't go to your grandfather's service."

"It's hardly the same thing. That was only Brisbane and I had my whole family there. You knew that. But this time, you'll be going alone. And I want to come with you—"

She shook her head. "You don't understand. I don't need anyone to hold my hand."

"Ava—"

"Because I'm not going." She read the shock on his startled features.

The disbelief. The incredulity. And the satisfaction of all those things was worth another swig of her wine.

He shook his head. "Don't be too hasty and decide something you might regret. Whatever happened, they were still your parents."

She snorted and just pulled the bottle closer so she could top up her glass. "Do not talk to me about what I should or should not do. My father died to me a long time ago. My mother with him. I'm over mourning their loss."

"But, there must be other family? Won't they need you there?"

"No." She stared blankly ahead, feeling the cold sweep of history hollow her out inside. It was always there, the barren hole lurking below the papered surface of her existence. Only now she could feel its yawning presence like the aching legacy that it was. "There's nobody."

"Oh, Ava."

She looked up at him, and the compassion in his eyes nearly brought her undone. Compassion she neither wanted nor needed, and making her want to lash out.

She didn't want anyone's pity. "I'm happy your family has given you more reason to mourn their loss than embrace it, but don't expect my family to be the same. Now, please go."

He stood and she felt a tide of relief flow over her. "I'll go," he said. "Can I call you tomorrow?"

"Why? You'll see me at the show."

"You're not seriously thinking of going?"

"I made a commitment. I'll be there. And now, do I really have to ask you again to leave?"

She heard the slide of the glass door and the crunch of his footsteps heading towards the driveway. She waited until she'd heard his car start, the roar of the engine, and then the sound of him disappearing out the driveway. And only then, when she could hear nothing but the rustle of gum leaves in the sleeping bush around her, did she open her eyes. Her empty glass stood before her and she reached for the bottle once again, and then stopped, and got to her feet.

It wasn't wine she needed right now. It was her work, and the time to think.

Time to revisit the past and nail that fucker shut.

And time to think about Caleb, and what she was going to do.

HE HATED LEAVING her that way. He drove down the windy road through the hills towards his flat in the suburbs feeling frustrated and impotent, all the while hating that once again she'd shut him out, excluding him from what it was that mattered in her life, as if he meant nothing. As if he couldn't be a friend when she was hurting.

And that was what he was. Maybe he didn't know when it quite happened, but he was damned sure that somewhere along the line they'd gone from being more than just casual fuckbuddies, to friends.

So why did she push him away?

Because of this damned arrangement of theirs? This casual hookup thing they had going? This no obligation, no commitment sex whenever it suited arrangement, based on mutual need and mutual convenience and nothing more, and the judges' decision is final and no correspondence will be entered into?

Well, that had been fine and dandy once before. That had suited them both. But twelve months on, he wasn't sure that was how he saw it anymore. He wasn't sure that was how he wanted it. Damn it, she meant something to him. He cared about her.

And, hell, maybe, just maybe, it was time to tell her that.

Without freaking her out and without making her think he wanted more. He didn't want to risk what they had when what they had was amazing.

But now he knew she was hurting, and he wanted to help.

He was worried about her, that was all.

That was all.

AVA NEVER WORKED if she'd been drinking. The level of realism in her art demanded her one hundred percent attention, a keen eye, and a skilful, sober hand. But tonight wasn't about realism.

Tonight was about emotion.

Unleashed, it poured in surround sound from the speakers, just as it poured pure and potent from her brush onto the canvas in broad slashes of paint until the canvas was a sea of darkness, an ominous, cave like room in a palace turned prison.

And there, in the centre, lay the princess, huddled on her side, her legs pulled up, her head curled into the arms crossed at chest, her fairy tale life in tatters.

Ava stood back then, letting her pumping heart slow, and finally gave way to the tears. But not for her dead father. Nor for her dead mother. But for the girl on the bed who could make no sense of it.

The girl who felt betrayed.

Abandoned.

Alone.

And no longer a princess, but an empty shell.

She blinked away the icy cold tears that streamed down her cheeks and turned to stand in the doorway, looking out over the black of the sleeping gorge to the perversely cheerful twinkling lights of the city beyond, and breathed deeply of the warm night air.

Was it any wonder she felt at home here, with the gorge and its deep, secret folds?

She took one last look at the canvas and sighed, knowing she needed to sleep if she was going to front up for a day painting faces at the show. Now she could.

Naked, she slipped into her bed with its ruffled sheets that still smelled of Caleb and sex. God, she would miss the sex.

He'd blown into her life on a blistering summer day and promised her nothing more than what she needed, hot sex and lots of it, and he'd delivered.

But lately lines seemed to be blurring.

And he was a good man. A strong man. A man who should have children one day and who would have by now, but for the mess of a failed marriage. This thing with her couldn't be long-term. He needed a woman without a past who could give him long-term.

She turned her face into the pillow, drinking in his scent.

Yes, she would miss the sex.

THE WEATHER FORECASTERS had got it right and they couldn't have had a better day for the annual Ashton Show. It had been forty degrees in the shade last year and every CFA and MFS guy there along with every local had one eye scanning the surrounding hills, and at least one nostril primed for smoke. Last year it had been so damned hot, it wasn't just the snags on the barbie that had been sizzling.

But today promised to max out at a near perfect twenty-eight degrees Celcius under a cloudless sky and that promised to bring the show's biggest crowds ever. Already before lunchtime they were doing brisk business with the barbeque. There was something about the smell of sizzling snags on a barbie that sure pulled the punters in.

Richo was wrangling the bacon and eggs on the next barbeque while Caleb tackled the sausages and onions. A couple of the junior members of the CFS crew were busy handling the orders and the cash before sending the customers Richo and Caleb's way to pick up their food. And just across the wide driveway that circled the football oval, across the groups of people wandering between the stalls and attractions around the perimeter, sat Ava at her small table stacked with face paints and a couple of chairs for her patrons, under a shady fold up umbrella.

She was busy today. Pretty much flat chat, and a lot busier than last year when they'd met, making Caleb wonder when he was ever going to get a chance to get a word with her. He couldn't leave things the way they were when they'd parted last night. He'd spent sleepless hours last night worrying about her and thinking about how wrong it was, the way they'd parted, and he couldn't bear to let it go any longer.

"Caleb!" Richo called.

"What?" Caleb came to, to find three teenaged boys waiting in front of his barbeque.

"Two sanger sandwiches with onion," Richo spelt out beside him. "And one without."

"Oh, sure," he said, and quickly loaded up three slices of bread with sausages. "Help yourself to sauce or mustard," he said, as he handed the plain one over before piling the other two with onions.

"Awesome!" said one of them, clearly an onion fan, before reaching for the sauce. "Thanks." The three moved off, munching on their sausage sangers, but a sudden rush of orders meant it was a good ten minutes before Caleb had a chance to check out what Ava was doing again. She'd finished on the little girl she'd been painting and was handing her the mirror so she could study her new face.

He couldn't make out what she said, but he could read her delight on her brightly painted face when she turned to her mother alongside. Another happy customer, he thought, as the recently painted butterfly took off excitedly for the next attraction, the vacated chair already taken by the next customer in line.

Damn but she was busy. But maybe if he could catch her eye, she might spare him five minutes? She had to have a break some time.

"Earth calling Caleb."

"What is it now?" he growled, because he checked and there were no waiting customers this time.

Richo chuckled, flipping eggs. "Boy, have you got it bad. Is she your girlfriend then?"

"What?"

"Come on! The one you were whistling about the other week. Is that her? Only you've been staring at her with puppy dog eyes all morning, and so I figured…"

"I have not been staring. I need to talk to her, that's all." And apologise for the dumb as shit way he'd tried to tell her how she should react to the news of the death of her parents.

It still blew him away that she'd been so blasé about their deaths, but she'd been right. He'd been reacting from his own worldly experience and it had never occurred to him that hers might have been different. Very much different by the way she'd reacted.

Meanwhile Richo just raised his eyebrows and flipped some bacon. "If you say so, buddy."

"And what's that supposed to mean?"

"Well," he said, adjusting the gas, "if I didn't know better, I reckon the last thing you've got on your mind is talking. I'd say that's a look of *lurve* you got going on there."

"Bullshit!" Caleb scoffed, topping up the sliced onions

on the plate to prepare for the next rush. "She's a friend, that's all." Nobody was supposed to know anything different and nobody would. They hadn't gone public with their relationship because it wasn't like it was a normal relationship. It was convenient for them both, that was all. Not to mention that it was nobody else's damn business. "I'm just worried about her."

Richo glanced through the strolling families and groups. "So what's wrong? She looks fine from where I'm standing. Real fine. One good-looking woman all right."

Caleb bristled, not sure he liked the idea of somebody else openly admiring Ava. But Richo was right. Her Eurasian good looks and her smile and the way she engaged with her small clients made her magnetic to children and adults alike. She came across as if she didn't have a care in the world. That was part of the problem. He looked over at his mate, wondering how much information was too much. And then he figured he'd had a gutful of keeping quiet and if it distracted Richo from all this ridiculous *lurve* talk… "Look, this is just between you and me right? But Ava just got word yesterday that her parents died in a car crash."

"Sheesh. Both of them? That's rough. Pretty amazing of her to even turn up today in that case."

"I know."

They both studied the smiling Ava a few seconds longer, Richo tugging on his ear lobe before he got back to work with his slide. "You sure wouldn't know she's just been dropped a bombshell like that. Nothing worse than a death in the family and having a funeral or two to look forward to."

"Yeah. Only she's not going."

"No? Her own parents, too."

"You see what I mean? Who doesn't go to their own mother and father's funeral?"

Richo shrugged, momentarily distracted as he filled an order for two bacon and egg sandwiches. "Bit weird, though. Most people go to catch up with the rest of the family."

"There's nobody else, she says. No family. No friends. No nothing."

Richo shook his head as he cracked a couple of eggs into rings on the sizzling plate. "Must have been a hell of a family bust up, in that case."

"Yeah," he said, chewing his bottom lip, "that's what I was thinking." But only after he'd gotten home and played it over in his mind a few times and realised was an ass hat he'd made of himself, telling her what to do like he knew all about it.

"Maybe you should try talking to her about it?"

"She won't and now she's pissed off with me and I really need to talk to her, but she's so busy painting faces."

"Well," said Richo, pointing with his tongs in Ava's direction, "there's your answer. Get in the queue."

Caleb blinked and looked at his mate for all of two seconds. "Here," he said, handing over his own tongs and pulling off his apron. "Cover for me."

Thirty seconds later he'd bought his ticket and was duly queued up in Ava's lineup. He didn't care he was the oldest one in the queue by a quarter century at least, not if it gave him an opportunity to talk to Ava.

She glanced up at the line as she finished off her current customer, her brows knitting when she saw him, before turning her attentions to the young boy at the head of the queue. "What would you like to be today?" she asked with a smile, as he sat down.

"A pirate," the boy said.

"Good choice," he heard Ava say, as she set to work.

One pirate, a tiger, and a rainbow princess later and it was Caleb's turn. He sat down on the kiddie-sized chair, praying it would take his weight.

"What are you doing, Caleb?" she asked, keeping her voice low as she washed her brushes.

"Getting my face painted, like everyone else in this lineup."

"You're not really here to have your face painted, though, are you?"

"Hey, I paid five bucks over the odds for this. I'm getting my face painted, just like everyone else in this queue."

She sighed, looked at the kids lined up behind him. "Some kids just never grow up," she told them, as she reached for her paints. "Okay, so what do you want to be?"

"Oh." He hadn't figured that far ahead.

One year ago he'd similarly had no idea and she'd chosen to paint his face so full of dark shadows, he'd come out looking uncannily like Hugh Jackman's Wolverine. He'd liked the look, but that was then and it would be a waste not to rock a different look this time.

"I'm not sure," he said. "I've seen a few superheroes wandering around today though." And that was the truth. A fair few Batmans and a Spiderman or three. He could live with being any other kind of superhero. "How about you choose something appropriate."

She raised her eyebrows at that and gave him his first smile, which he took as a win. Richo had been so right.

"Okay. Close your eyes for me."

A few seconds later he felt the damp of the sponge against his skin, and he knew she'd be applying a base colour. "So what are you going to paint me as?"

"Wait and see."

He could wait. Especially if it gave him the opportunity to talk to her. "How are you feeling today?"

"Fine," she said, without telling him anything at all, the sponge patting at his eyelids and over his eyebrows.

"I was worried about you last night."

"There was no need to be worried. Sit still."

It was no hardship sitting still. It allowed him to concentrate on the feel of the stroke of her sponge and then the brush against his skin, the long sweeping lines, the short stab of dots. He had no idea what superhero she was painting him up as, but he had Ava sitting before him and right now that was all he cared about. He didn't have to crack open an eyelid to know she was right there, intently staring at his face as she worked. So close he could smell the verbena scent of the soap and shampoo she favoured. And after a couple of hours with nothing but the smell of frying bacon, onion, and sausages in his nostrils, that was enough right there to give him a hard-on, even without the sensual stroking of her brush. And coupled with the brushstrokes… His whole body hummed… "You know what that brush of yours does to me, don't you?"

Her hand stalled, mid-stroke. Yeah, she knew, because he'd told her the first time they'd spent the night together.

"This is a family show, Caleb," she warned, keeping her voice low, as she resumed her work on his face, his forehead this time. "There are children present."

"I know. That's not why I wanted to see you, anyway." He sucked in a breath, shifted his voice lower. "I was hoping we could talk some time later. Maybe I could drop by your place, or you could come to my place and I'll fix us something to eat."

"Call out for pizza, you mean?" she scoffed, hard at work on his cheek.

"Like I said, I'll fix us something to eat."

He heard a ripple of laughter coming from somewhere behind him and figured one of the mums in the queue must have overheard and enjoyed his joke. "Okay, you're done," she said, with a decisive dab of her brush, a final full stop to her work, "I'll meet you at your place. If you still want me to come, that is. You can open your eyes now."

He blinked, wondering why she'd qualify her agreement while his eyes took a moment to adjust to the bright daylight. Of course he wanted her to come.

She handed him the mirror. "Take a look."

He took the mirror and lifted it to his face, and blinked again. Because what used to be his face was now a sea of pink and white and sparkles. Sparkles?

"You gave me sparkles?" And on his cheek was a dark splotch of pink with what looked like eyes. He angled the mirror to look closer at the abomination. "What the hell is that?"

And a little girl's voice cried, "It's Peppa Pig!" And the ripples of laughter around him grew louder.

He looked at Ava, aghast. "I thought at least you were going to make me into some kind of superhero."

"Oh, ask anyone in this line and I think you'll find she is," she said, as she wiped her hands on a cloth, and, damn her to hell and back, but she was enjoying this. "Maybe next time you should be more specific."

"But—"

"Off you go, Peppa Pig, I've got customers waiting."

"I want to be Peppa Pig too," said the little girl up next to her mum. "Ple-ease!"

"And me," said another.

It didn't matter how many little girls wanted to look just like him, it was like the walk of shame going back to the barbeque, there was no way he could hide so much sparkles and pink, no way he didn't draw the attention of every person going by.

"About time you got back," Richo said, his back to him, busy juggling tongs and a slide. "It's gone bloody gang-busters since you left." He turned to pass Caleb the tongs, took one look at his face and cracked up. "What the fuck happened to you? You look like some kind of nightmare on pink street."

He pointed to his cheek. "This is Peppa Pig, if you don't mind. Apparently some kind of superhero. Apparently."

Richo just guffawed. "Has Dylan got wind of this yet?" Richo had been on the Hazmat course Dylan had given the week he'd arrived and Caleb was always a bit wary about the easy rapport he seemed to share with his brother.

"Nope, and I'd really prefer he—"

Quick as a flash, Richo pulled out his phone and snapped off a couple of shots before Caleb could finish what he was saying, let alone get his hands in front of his face, his so called mate already thumbing his way onto social media. "He's sure going to. As will everyone else at the station. This one's going straight to the pool room!"

Bloody hell. Caleb was never going to live this down. But at least as he went back to wielding the tongs on the sausage sizzle, he knew he hadn't blown it completely. He was going to see Ava again. The humiliation was almost worth it.

His phone beeped and he checked the screen and saw incoming from his brother. A single word.

BAHAHAHAHAHAHA!

And Caleb pocketed his phone and sighed. Yeah, almost worth it.

Chapter Six

H IS PLACE WASN'T much, just a modest nineteen sixties red brick two-bedroom unit in a group of four just down on the suburbs at the foot of the hills, but after his divorce and Angie getting the house, he hadn't been left with a whole lot of money for anything fancier. It had taken a while to get over the move into a smaller space, but now he appreciated how much better it suited him. He was close to his station and the spare bedroom was big enough to house his bench press along with his various fitness bikes, for when he wanted a fast ride through the suburbs down to the beach and back, or a tough ride through on a cross country track through the hills.

And the bonus was, there was nobody to complain whatever he chose.

Now he had his favourite album – *Californication* – playing softly on the stereo. He'd picked a sprig of flowers off the tree out back by the carport that was sitting in a glass of water – Angie had taken all the vases – and the dinner he'd picked up ready and waiting. By the time he heard her small hatchback pull up in the visitor park outside, he had a knot the size of Tasmania in his gut.

For despite the playful banter between them today at the show, things had changed between them lately, he knew.

And it wasn't just because of that phone call last night. All that had done was draw an underline under what he already knew. Things were different now.

Even the night of the crash, he'd sensed something was wrong. Sure they'd made love, but Ava had seemed withdrawn and on edge and he had a feeling it wasn't just about the painting that was giving her grief.

He met her at the door. "You washed your face," she said, as she stepped inside.

"Reluctantly," he lied, as he reached down to kiss her. She turned her face at the last moment – intentionally? – and his lips brushed against her cheek and he knew he had a lot of ground to make up.

"Thai?" she said, sniffing the air appreciatively as she headed for the table, looping her bag over the back of the chair.

"I lied about the pizza. Hope you're not disappointed."

"And flowers too," she said, noticing his feeble attempt at table decoration. "I love frangipani flowers," she said, lifting the glass and inhaling deeply the scent of the yellow and white flowers. "So bold and beautiful." He watched as she traced the petals with the tip of one finger. "I tried once, but they won't grow up in the hills where I am."

"Take it. There's a whole tree out back covered in flowers if you want."

She smiled then, as she thanked him and sat down, but it was a low wattage smile, measured like it was being rationed, and that failed to brighten his mood, and he decided there was nothing for it but to come right out and tell her what he'd wanted to ever since he'd realised he'd been such a complete jerk.

"Look, Ava," he said, as they sat down at his small table for two with the phad thai and red duck curry and steamed rice sitting between them, like it was just like any other night, when clearly it wasn't. Things had changed, and it made him nervous and more conscious than ever of not stuffing tonight up too. "I want to apologise for coming across so heavy-handed last night. You were right; I was coming from a different place. I should never have assumed your situation was the same or that your feelings might mirror my own. It was wrong of me to assume, and to badger you that way, and all I did was upset you more. I'm sorry."

She nodded. Her answering smile tweaking the corners of her lip, though not enough to make him relax. "Thank you. I'm sorry too, that our night had to end that way. But, it's done."

As easily as that? He watched her spoon rice and curry onto her plate, wondering at her ability to shut down a conversation, to not let him get close to understanding as they made small talk about the food, the spices, and the wine. This bloody dance they were doing. Knowing but not knowing. Lovers sharing bodies but not minds.

It was killing him that she kept the barricades up, that she wouldn't let him in. That she stepped a foot back if he stepped so much as an inch forward.

Should he tell her he cared, and that maybe if she only shared what it was that was troubling her, that he might be able to help? Would she open up or would she close the door on their not-quite-a-relationship altogether?

There was only one way to find out, but knowing it might mean the end held him in check. Then again, she was here, tonight, and surely that meant something. So in the end he bit his tongue and chased curry and noodles around his plate, only half tasting the food.

When it had all turned to custard with Angie, when things had changed, he hadn't fought it. He'd been just as guilty in their breakup and he'd let it slide. He hadn't cared enough to save it.

He cared about losing Ava, though. Maybe because one year of casual hookups wasn't anywhere near long enough to have had enough of her. His marriage had soured in the space of two. Maybe the novelty took longer to wear off when you didn't live with someone day after day, although he couldn't imagine ever getting sick of waking up to this woman.

"That was delicious, thank you," said Ava, putting down

her fork and leaning back in her chair.

He smiled tightly. At least he hadn't managed to stuff up dinner. "Least I could do. Anything you'd like to do now?" he said, collecting dishes to rinse in the sink. "Watch a movie or maybe go for a walk?" He had the distinct impression she wasn't looking for sex.

"Neither. Caleb, forget the dishes. Come and sit back down. We need to talk."

A cannonball lodged in his gut. He turned to face her, to try to read her. She was so composed. Eerily composed. It was almost like she had an aura around her tonight, or a layer of armour plating that he couldn't breach.

He sat down opposite her. "I'm listening."

"What we have," she started, "this thing between us, is special. I know I can call on you and you can call on me, and if it suits"—she shrugged—"well, then we can get together and it's good."

"Better than good," he said, already not liking the way this conversation was heading.

She nodded. "Better than good, true. But what we have, it's also fragile. It is what it is. It can't be more than that, it can't be bigger, or it will shatter. And, just lately, I've been worried." She took a breath and Caleb held his. "I never thought that we might still be seeing each other after a year. And I wondered…" Her eyes glowed softly in the light. Sadly. "Lately, I've been wondering if one year was too long."

Air hissed through his teeth. "Is that why you came tonight. To tell me we're finished?"

She reached across the table and took his hand and laced her fingers through his. "No. Because I thought about it, and I'm not ready for it to end yet. I'm selfish and I'm not ready to pop this fragile bubble that we share. Not if we don't have to." She squeezed his fingers. "Do you understand?"

His head was spinning from the sudden change of direction, relief coming so close after the sucker punch of thinking she was ending it. He nodded as he drank in her perfect features, eyes the colour of liqueur brandy lit by firelight, a nose with just the right amount of kink to make it more real, more perfect, and a full mouth that could switch from sweet to sinful in an instant, and he knew he wasn't ready to lose her. One year with this woman was nowhere near enough.

"You want things to stay exactly the way they are."

"Yes. And I want *us* to stay the way *we* are, two individual people who meet up occasionally for mutual pleasure, whether that be sex or a meal or both, nothing more. And I realise I'm guilty of blurring the lines too. Getting you to pose for me – mixing pleasure with business – I realise that was a mistake." She nodded. "But if this thing between us is to continue, that's how it has to work. That's all it can ever be. Agreed?"

Caleb wasn't a man who was used to being dictated to. Angie had tried that – Angie of the complaints about his shift work and demands for him to spend more time with her, and in the end, Angie of the ultimatum – the job or her, and look where that had got her? But he also knew that a man would have to be a fool to say no to Ava, whatever her demands. A man would have to be a fool to argue that it wasn't enough, that he wanted more, that he wanted to crack the door open and be let inside her world, because he then would lose her entirely, while at least this way, he would have part of her, for however long it lasted.

And never before had he been so sorely tempted to agree with anyone. His fingers clenched and unclenched while his mind battled with the insoluble dilemma.

Because he also knew that a man would also be a fool not to acknowledge that just having Ava wasn't enough. That he wanted her on his terms too, not only within the confines of the strict boundaries on which she insisted.

His voice, when it came, was mired in the agony of a difficult choice. "No."

"What?"

"I said, no," he repeated, feeling stronger for it, knowing he was being honest with himself and with her. "I don't agree."

"But that's the way it has to be. That's what we agreed, remember? That's what we both wanted."

"Sure, that's exactly what I had wanted – then. But that was a year ago. Now, like it or not, agreement or not, I want more."

Her eyes were wide, cognac-coloured pools of disbelief. "You can't mean that. I thought—"

And suddenly he couldn't sit any more. He sprang up from the table, pacing into the kitchen and back. "You thought I'd be happy being put back in my box, being brought out on special occasions or when it suited you? You thought I'd accept your crazy conditions without questioning them? This is killing me, Ava. I can't go on this way. I don't understand why we have to. We know each other enough by now to know we're good together, so why do we have to put limitations on it?"

She blinked up at him. "I can't..."

"You can't, or you won't?"

"I..." she said, getting to her feet, the chair scraping across the wooden floor, the discordant sound in tune with his jarred senses. She shook her head. "I'm sorry. I should go."

"You don't have to. This doesn't have to be the end. Not unless that's what you want – what you really want."

She collected her bag and cradled it in her arms against her chest. "You don't give me much choice."

He growled out a sigh as he raked his fingers through his short hair. "Don't put this back on me. Think about it, Ava. I'll give you space and time and you can think on it. Think about us."

"Thank you for dinner," was all she said, as she headed for her car.

He collected the flowers from the glass, adding another couple of sprigs freshly picked from the tree, and met her at her car.

"Thank you," she said, once again putting the flowers to her face and breathing in the heady fragrance.

"You're not too tired to drive?"

She smiled wearily as she placed the flowers on the passenger seat. "It's not far. Goodbye."

And then he watched the taillights of her hatchback disappear down the street, wondering if tonight was their last together. One year ago today, give or take, they'd got together and damned near combusted when they had. One year later and they hadn't even kissed. Talk about a lousy anniversary.

He rubbed the back of his neck as he headed back inside and smelt the scent of the frangipani on his hands and thought about the lonely nights stretching out before him with no Ava in his life.

But then, she'd never really been there.

AVA NEVER SAW it coming.

She'd felt drained as she drove away. Totally exhausted. After barely sleeping last night and working all today in the sun at the show, it had taken every last shred of energy she'd possessed to be able to hold her nerve with Caleb.

And, for a moment there, after she'd laid out the ground

rules, she'd almost sworn that he was on the same page, and that she'd secured his agreement. But then he'd turned the tables on her, and suddenly he'd been the one calling the shots.

Why had he done that, when he knew what would have to happen?

Why had he insisted it wasn't enough, when it was all it could ever be?

Sure, she'd been as much to blame for letting Caleb get too close. Those sketches had blurred the lines between them, smudging the boundaries just as she smudged the images of him in charcoal on the page. She'd let her excitement for the collection rule her head.

Stupid.

But she'd expected him to understand. She'd expected him to back off. All tonight was supposed to be was a timely reminder of the boundaries. A circuit breaker, that was all.

She hadn't expected him to be the one to pull the pin on their affair.

"Think about it," he'd said, when there was nothing to think about. She'd learned something since that naïve girl of sixteen and her equally stupid twenty-year-old self. She'd learned to take care of herself and her career. She'd learned to take control of her own destiny.

And nobody was taking that away from her ever again.

The narrow ribbon of road followed the creek bed, wending its way through the sparsely populated valley floor.

Soon she'd be home and she could crawl into her bed. She felt sleep tugging at her now, weighing down her eyelids. Not long to go. She rounded a bend, confused to see two glowing lights ahead where there should be none. She was almost upon them when she realised and she slammed her foot on the brake, all the gear that she'd taken to the show, the paints and chairs and umbrella that she hadn't bothered to unpack yet, crashing into the back of her seat with the sudden deceleration.

The car skidded to a stop, just inches short of the beast. The kangaroo jerked upright, looking confused, the spell the headlights had held it in broken, before it turned its head and bounded gracefully away, disappearing into the bush at the edge of the road.

She rested there with her head on the steering wheel a few moments, while she caught her breath and her thudding heart slipped from her throat back into her chest. Then she glanced over at the tangled mess of her gear behind her. There was a job for tomorrow, but it could have been a lot worse. At least she hadn't hit it. At least they were both okay. She put the car into gear, scanning the surroundings as best she could, to make sure the kangaroo or any of its friends wasn't sitting there, waiting to jump out and scare the living daylights out of her again, and slowly drove home.

But at least now she didn't have to worry about falling asleep.

After that little heart starter, she was wide awake.

CALEB DIDN'T HAVE to work at giving Ava space. A call out to a fire in a massive pile of recycled building material and timber offcuts at a recycling facility took care of that. A worker who'd attempted to put out the fire with a garden variety fire extinguisher before it had engulfed the pile and sent him fleeing for his life claimed it had been sparked by an electrical fault on his tractor, and in no time at all the fire quickly took hold, spreading to a nearby stockpile of tyres before the first of the firefighters had arrived.

By the time Caleb's crew had been called in a couple of hours later, the fire was already the size of a city office block, the flames shooting tens of metres into the sky.

It was the biggest industrial fire ever seen in the city, crews from all over the metropolitan area involved, and the only blessing was it was in an area fringed with open land so it couldn't spread into the suburbs. For three days and nights more than one hundred fireys battled to contain the fire, the heat generated by the flames so intense it seemed to absorb the retardant and water poured onto it before they could act to cool the fire down, while the thick pillar of black smoke that snaked upwards into the sky prompted the health authorities to issue warnings to people in the surrounding suburbs with asthma and other chronic conditions to get the hell away or stay inside. Even despite their breathing equipment, more than a dozen firefighters had to be hospitalised for breathing difficulties.

Eventually the fire had burned down enough that big earthmovers could be brought in to shift the burning material into smaller piles that could be tackled separately, but it would be days before the fire was completely mopped up.

It was a weary and filthy crew that headed back to the station after being stood down the final day but Caleb was proud of each and every one of them and the way they'd performed. Mike came out to greet them. "I've been hearing stellar reports about you guys."

"The crew did well, all of them," Caleb said, "and this guy –" he patted Matt on the back – "did an awesome job. That was a tough gig for an experienced officer, let alone a rookie. Talk about a trial by fire."

"Thanks," the still teen-aged rookie said, and Caleb would swear he was blushing under the grime on his face.

"I look forward to hearing all about it. Now go get cleaned up, you lot. There's pizza in the kitchen."

"Do you mind if I don't stay for pizza?" asked Matt. "Only my mum—" He stopped there, biting his lip, clearly thinking he'd said too much.

"Your mum will have been worried sick about you," Mike said. "Go set her mind at rest that you're okay."

Right now Caleb wondered if he'd ever be able to smell anything but the stench of burning tyres again. Bone weary now the adrenaline rush of fighting the fire was past, he hit the showers, managed to inhale four pieces of pizza and hefty chunk of garlic bread, and was home within the hour.

The lawn under the tree out behind the carport – frangipani, she'd called it – was white with scattered petals of fallen flowers, and he thought of Ava then, as he climbed from his car. He rubbed his aching head. Well, she should be happy. She sure couldn't accuse him of overstepping any boundaries lately.

He was zoning out in front of the telly when the text came. He picked up his phone, and blinked when he saw the message was from Ava.

*Were you **at** that fire?*

> *Yes.*

Are you okay?

> *I'm fine.*

Two minutes later came the response.

That's good.
Are you busy?

> *Dead on my feet.*

Of course.
Sleep well.

He stared at the messages until his screen went blank and then he let his hand and the phone flop onto his chest.

Interesting.

AVA CIRCLED SLOWLY around her studio, a mug of ginger tea cradled in her hands. She knew not to feel disappointed, but it was impossible not to feel relieved. She'd seen the thick, black column of smoke rising for days from the industrial area near the swampy saltbush land of the port, and she'd wondered whether he'd been caught up fighting it.

But he was okay and knowing that was enough. Sure, it would have been nice to share this moment with someone, especially someone who'd seen this collection develop and knew how much work had gone into it. Especially someone who'd been part of its inspiration. But after the way they'd parted the other night, maybe this was better. She didn't want Caleb getting the wrong idea.

All around her, on the walls of the studio on the floor and sofa were displayed the thirty artworks she'd be exhibiting – everything else, the also rans, the unfinished works in progress and the picture she'd done in a frenzy of rage and turmoil on the night she'd learned her parents had died, put to one side. It was the first time she'd arranged the entire collection together. The first time she'd been able to assess if it worked as a collection or needed something added or subtracted or tweaked. But all around her was colour and texture, the lushness of plump ripe fruit against the bold colours of bowls and jugs, the richly textured midnight blue velvet remnant that she'd pulled from a suitcase and even the rustic terracotta tiles of her floor. And then there were the stunning charcoal renditions of Caleb's sculpted body.

And without a shred of false modesty, and she knew they all worked brilliantly together – and that was here, scattered around the walls of her studio. Adorning the walls of Evan's gallery, they'd look even better.

No wonder the blood in her veins almost fizzed. Now she only had to work out a name for the collection. She'd been intending to call it *Harvest* because of the fruit and vegetables that featured so predominantly in her work – but then there were now the pictures of Caleb too, to consider.

She moved in front of the series of four – of him standing with his back to her right here in this studio, of him in the shower under a stream of water, and one of him pulling on a shirt over his shoulders, and finally, the one of him lying satiated and spent across her rumpled bed – and she could feel the irresistible tug of his physicality, the tight bunches of his muscles, the corded strength in his neck and the sculpted washboard of his abs, and it surprised her how much they reminded her of making love with him and how much she wanted to right now.

And it came to her then, the only name the exhibition could be.

Texture.

And she picked up her phone again to call him up to tell him, when she stopped herself short. And she called another number on her phone, and waited impatiently for it to be picked up.

"Evan," she said, when it was, and because she'd needed

to tell somebody, "I've got great news."

THE NEXT DAY at the station was filled with routine upon routine. There was a shit load of stuff that needed cleaning and restocking after the huge fire, and Caleb spent what felt like a heap of time filling out reports too, all of which some desk jockey at head office would collate and pull together so the industrial waste fire and response could be analysed and picked apart so they could learn what worked and what didn't and do better next time. And while it was a bit of a pain doing the reports, getting the results was another one of the things about this job Caleb loved. You never stopped learning. You never stopped getting prepared for the next incident.

And routine felt pretty good right now. It had been an exhausting and testing few days after which routine was a welcome change. It was luxury to have time to catch up and think. And Ava's texts were part of the mix, and every now and then they'd do another lap around his head. Had she seen the smoke and the reports in the news, to reach out to him that way? Had she heard some firefighters had needed to be taken to hospital and she'd been worried about him?

Had she'd gone away to think like he'd asked her to?

God, so long as he lived, he'd never understand women.

Mike came looking for Caleb right about the time he was getting changed to knock off.

Mike leaned up against the door frame of the change room. "Couple of things I've got to tell you," he said, his face serious. "I've had word from above that this investigation into the Victorian bushfires might be coming to an end. Looks like they'll be making a report in a couple of months or so."

Caleb's ears pricked up, searching Mike's words for any hint of optimism, finding none. "And?" he prompted.

"That's all I've got."

"There's no word on any preliminary findings yet?"

"Not that anyone's telling me." He sighed. "Sorry, Caleb. I know how wrong it is – Leonard Knight was a bloody legend, for god's sake. To go out with this hanging over his head…" He shook his head.

Caleb nodded. Yeah, well, they'd waited this long for a result already. It would be worth the wait if their grandfather was cleared.

He stood up to go. "Thanks Mike. See you when I'm back on deck."

But Mike wasn't going anywhere. He shuffled on the spot where he stood. "You might want to sit down again. There's something else."

"Oh?"

"I've had a call," he said, the creased lines around his eyes looking that bit deeper. "From Dave O'Dwyer – the husband of that crash victim you cut out the wreck. He's ready to meet you now."

Caleb sat down on a long sigh. So it was going to happen then? Because sometimes people said they wanted to meet up afterwards – after the formalities and sometimes the funeral – and then they got on with life, and they either forgot or they didn't want to go back. It didn't bother Caleb whichever it was because it was their loss, their grief and if they wanted to leave it there, that was fine. He'd just happened to be there on the day when their lives had unexpectedly intersected. He'd just been doing his job and it hadn't just been him. There'd been a whole team working to save lives.

"What about the rest of crew?"

Mike rapped his knuckles on the door frame. "I know, I know. But he just wants you apparently. Got something to talk to you about, one-on-one. He wants to set up a time for tomorrow." Mike looked a bit sheepish then. "I did warn him that you were starting four days off…"

Caleb sighed, knowing it was going to be heartrending whenever it happened, so the sooner the better as far as he was concerned. "If it suits, I can be there at ten."

Which was how Caleb found himself the next morning, knocking on a door next to a dying pot plant on the front verandah of a tiny terrace house in the inner suburb of Norwood.

A barefoot, frazzled-looking guy opened the door wearing shorts and a messy T-shirt with a tea towel slung over his shoulder. He looked weary, like he hadn't slept for a month and Caleb knew he had damned good reason.

"You're Caleb Knight?" the man said, and for a moment he just stood there and stared at Caleb, and in the man's eyes Caleb saw a world of pain and loss. Then he gave a bitter-sweet smile while he wiped his hands on the tea towel before thrusting out his hand. "I'm Dave. Thank you so much for coming," he said, before pulling him into a stiff man hug.

Caleb knew he was in trouble. He was already choking up and he hadn't even got inside the door.

"Come and meet the little guy," Dave said, leading Caleb into a family room peppered with shoes and abandoned toys while on the table sat a basket piled high with laundry.

In the kitchen in the corner the remnants of breakfast were littered all over the bench. And there, on the other side of the room stood the bassinet.

Dave rounded the basket, his hands on the side of the bassinet, gently rocking it. "He's sleeping now, thank god. Took me ages to get him settled after the school run, but finally he's asleep and I can get something done." He looked around the room. "Sorry about the state of the place," he said. "I'm not too good at keeping house."

Caleb shook his head, not bothered in the least, and staring down at the tiny creature in the bassinet, the cupid bow of his mouth, the nub of nose and the even tinier fingers wrapped around his turned down sheet.

"He was three weeks prem, but he's doing well. He's a tough little bugger, that's for sure."

Caleb nodded, searching for something to say. "I don't

know much about babies, but this one looks pretty good."

"You don't have kids?"

"No." He'd always imagined he'd have a clutch of kids by now.

His mum had been hoping for grandchildren from the day he and Angie married. But those dreams had turned to dust with his divorce, and with neither him nor his brother looking like hooking up with someone permanent, their mum was going to have to go on hoping.

"We've got three," Dave said. "Sylvie's six and Anthony's five and just started school. Makes for some interesting mornings," he added, with a hollow laugh that ended with him blinking his eyes and reaching for his tea towel as he turned away.

It was excruciating. God only knew how the man coped.

"Anyway," he said, clearing his throat as he moved to the mantelpiece nearby and picked up a picture.

A smiling woman looked out of the photo. Caleb barely recognised her, he'd been concentrating on getting her out and the ambos had had her all masked up while he'd worked, but the brunette hair – yeah – he remembered that. And he remembered the ambos talking urgently to each other. He remembered their desperate, "We're losing her." He remembered wielding the Jaws of Life like it was his own loved one – his own wife – trapped inside the mangled wreck, battling the twisted metal. Battling time. He remembered the, "She's gone," and Caleb's gut descending to the depths of despair. Caleb closed his eyes. There were some things you should be able to forget.

Dave smiled down at the picture. "Sally was such a great mum. She loved the kids so much. And, boy," he said, looking around again, "she'd sure go ape if she saw how I've let the house go—"

His words stalled. This time he didn't bother trying to hide the tears. Carefully, almost reverently, he put the photo back on the mantel and placed his fingers on another, of his wife, with their two children in her arms and sitting on a horse drawn tram. Victor Harbor, he recognised, with Granite Island behind. His folks had taken Dylan and him there once for a family holiday when they were kids. Happy memories, only now there would be no happy family shots of the five of this family. No more pictures of Sally with her arms around three kids this time.

"Oh, god, sorry," Dave said with a sniff, returning to the bassinet. "I didn't ask you over so I could cry all over you."

"It's okay," Caleb said, his throat suddenly two sizes too small, cursing himself for not being able to save her.

Cursing a drunk nineteen-year-old who'd got his girl-friend to drive and who'd subsequently been charged with two counts of manslaughter, but that was hardly going to help this man now. He watched Dave return to the bassinet, his fingers stroking the sleeping baby's brow, his grief palpable.

"Anyway," he said, smiling down at the sleeping baby,

"Sally and I had the name picked out. We knew it was a boy. We'd spent entire evenings going through all the baby name books until we finally settled on one we both liked. Harry Alexander O'Dwyer.

"We were all ready for the big day. Sally could hardly wait. And then – well you were there, you know what happened. And the silly thing is, she shouldn't have been there. She only went out for milk. I'd had a couple of beers with dinner and she wouldn't let me go. Joked that it was her last chance to drive while she could still fit behind the wheel."

Caleb closed his eyes against the sheer dumb luck of it all. He hadn't known that bit. Imagined being in his place and didn't know how this man would ever forgive himself for that. The baby sighed in its sleep and Caleb sighed with it. Damn straight.

"Anyway," Dave continued, "I know Sal's somewhere up there smiling down on the kids and no doubt scowling at me for being such a shit housekeeper, but when the doctors operated on Sal and when they let me see him in the crib for the first time, and he wrapped his tiny hand around my finger – I knew she'd be with me one hundred per cent agreement on this."

A tear fell on the baby's cheek, its long eyelashes twitched in slumber, and his father quickly brushed it away with the pad of his thumb and turned his tear streaked face up to Caleb. "He wouldn't be here if it wasn't for you, I could have lost them both that night. I would have, if you hadn't got her out in time to save the baby. So we've called him Caleb, after you. Caleb Harry. It's a good name."

Caleb had trouble with his vision after that. Somehow he managed to blunder his way back to his car, and turn his head towards the roof, needing time to think. The man had lost his wife, and he was thanking him.

And he needed – he needed…

He reached for his phone, punched Ava's name, impatient for her to pick up. He knew it wasn't too soon. Her texts told him it was okay to call. Her voice was husky when she picked up, like she'd been working late last night and sleeping in, like she often did.

"I need to see you."

"Yes," she said, after a moment's hesitation. "When."

"Now."

"Okay."

"And Ava?"

"Yes?"

"Don't bother getting dressed."

THIS WAS WHAT she wanted from him, she thought, her fingers curled in his hair as he tripped every nerve ending in her body with his clever tongue, this passionate whirlwind of sexual pleasure. He'd arrived less than half an hour after his call and torn off his clothes and promptly buried his face between her legs and sent her senses and her heart rate soaring.

This was how things should be.

And then she stopped thinking, and gave herself up to the wave of pleasure that rolled over her, higher and higher as it approached the shore, until it crashed on the sandy beach, leaving her gasping for air. He kissed his way up her humming body then, raining kisses over her sweated skin, and, with a cry half victory, half anguish, buried himself deep inside her.

There was no reprieve and no time to come down before he was taking her right back up again, his powerful thrusts urging her on to catch onto the second wave and ride that one too, all the way up to the dizziest of heights before, with one final thrust, the wave crashed beneath them and she clung to him as they fell together, spinning into the foaming wash.

Oh, yes, she thought with his sweat slickened body slumped over hers, this was what she wanted from Caleb. Nothing more. Nothing less.

IT WAS GOOD to be back in Ava's bed. He lay on his back with Ava curled against him. He leaned over and kissed the dark curtain of her hair, breathing in her scent. It felt good. It felt right. And now his body was sated and his mind was resting. Blank.

Except for one tiny thing with long eyelashes and a cupid's bow mouth.

When had he stopped wanting kids? When had that dream died? When he'd divorced Angie, or before, during those troubled years when the thought of bringing another life into their tortured world was anathema to him, even when she'd begged him and said it would help, that it would bring them closer together?

Why fuck up some poor kid's life, he'd reasoned, when your marriage was already heading for the rocks? And then, in the aftermath, he'd been so relieved to put that era behind him, he'd forgotten.

He breathed in deeply and blew out on a sigh. On the air, he could smell the scent of frangipani flowers that she'd put in a vase by the side of the bed. Half of them had fallen off, some of them lying on the wooden bedside table, the edges of the snowy white petals turning brown. Alongside him, Ava stirred briefly and settled back into a doze. He was thirty-two already. Three quarters of the way to the big four-oh, when it all came down to it. If he was going to have kids before he was too old, if he was going to show them the tracks and cliffs and caves he and Dylan had scrambled over as kids, or take them on holidays before he was on a zimmer frame and too old to enjoy it, maybe he ought to think about it.

It would sure make Mum happy too. She'd be all over grandkids. Dad too, for that matter.

One day, he might want to think about it.

Idly, he stroked Ava's arm with his thumb, thinking about her at the show. Ava was good with kids and they loved her. She'd smiled and chatted and sent every kid away happy. Their kids would look pretty cute too, he figured especially a girl. She'd be a stunner like her mum, no doubt.

Didn't Ava want kids one day? He'd always assumed wanting kids was pre-programmed into women's DNA, a bit like he'd always figured he'd have his own one day without knowing the detail. It would happen. It was the natural progression of events. Like Monday turning into Tuesday and not skipping direct to Saturday.

Not that there was any chance of having kids with Ava. Not the way she was determined to keep their relationship strictly at arm's length, even while they were busy shagging each other stupid. It was some kind of miracle he was back in her bed at all. He could just imagine how she'd take the news he was even thinking about babies. He snorted and sighed again.

Still, shame.

Ava stirred at his snort. "Wha-?" she said, sleepily, blinking.

"Coffee?" he asked, his stomach rumbling up a storm and thinking it was almost lunch time.

She nodded, sweeping her long hair from her face as she sat up, "Mm, please."

"Be right back, in that case."

He eased out of the bed and watched as she stretched her arms up high, long slender limbs that moved with catlike grace as she stretched away her sleep and Caleb shook his head as he headed for the kitchen. Yeah, bloody shame.

Ten minutes later, coffee in hand, she showed him her studio with the artworks for the collection all on display. "What do you think?"

He walked in a circle on the spot, sensing the excitement in her voice and the way she held herself in her blue dressing gown, arms crossed as if holding her breath while she waited for his reaction. She needn't have worried. He didn't know a hell of a lot about art, but he knew what she had was amazing. Even the four of him in various stages of undress – including the one of him on the bed, where she'd included a sizeable slice of his butt cheeks—he couldn't remember agreeing to that, but he was pretty impressed she'd managed that from memory—worked in with the whole. "You've nailed it, Ava."

"I think so too," she admitted, taking a sip from her mug. "Two weeks early too. That's a record for me."

"So what does your agent think?"

Her head tilted to the side. "What makes you think I have an agent?"

He shrugged, taking his time to look at each of the pictures in more detail. "I dunno. I assumed all artists had agents – to handle all the admin and organise stuff like exhibitions or something."

"No," she said tightly, rearranging the order of some of the paintings. "I had one. It didn't work out."

"Fair enough," he said, wandering around the space, finding the one with the lemons she'd had trouble with that night and that now looked almost three dimensional, it was so real.

And just behind was stack of canvases stacked together, and what he saw there made him frown. He'd got used to Ava's style, the detailed, precise brushstrokes, and this was something completely different. It was dark and ominous, the strokes of the paint like mad slashes across the canvas, and there in the centre – he peered closer – was a naked figure curled up in the foetal position on a bed, and, for the life of him, he'd almost swear it was Ava.

"I haven't seen this one before."

"What?" she said, looking around. "No!" She abandoned her rearranging, rushing to his side, wrestling the canvas away from him, turning it around and shuffling others behind it. More still lifes, he noticed the others were, and they were good too, though maybe lacking the same vibrancy as the others she'd included in the collection. But there was nothing like that first, mad one.

"Not that one. It's rubbish."

"The girl on the bed – she looked like you."

"Don't be ridiculous." She tucked hair behind her ears, then wrapped her arms around her. "It was an experiment. I was trying something different." She screwed up her nose. "It didn't work out."

"Fine," he said with his hands in the air. It was no skin off his nose. He was only asking, even if it did look like her.

"I'm sorry," she said, "it's embarrassing for people to see work that isn't up to scratch."

And then she smiled, placing her hands on his naked chest and her lips curled up provocatively. "And now, I need to have a shower. Care to join me?"

There were times when Caleb didn't think about whether to answer in the affirmative, and being asked by a woman to share her shower – especially when she was this woman – was right up there on the list. And Caleb decided that there were more important things in life than lunch and his rumbling stomach and the mystery that was this woman.

At least, for now.

Chapter Seven

CALEB HAD JUST finished sweating up a storm in the gym and was about to hit the showers when Mike gathered the shift together for an impromptu group meeting. A shower would have to wait. He slung his towel around his neck and joined Richo at the back of the group.

"Listen up everyone," Mike said in his booming voice when everyone was present. "I'm sorry for the short notice but I'm looking for some volunteers to help out at a function tomorrow night."

"That'd be right," grumbled Richo, rolling his eyes in Caleb's direction, clearly worrying about losing valuable time when he could be at the pub chatting up the ladies, but Caleb was too busy hanging out for what was coming next to react. Tomorrow night was Ava's show, and he had a horrible suspicion…

"This is all for a worthy cause, I can assure you. Most of you will probably have heard of local Adelaide Hills artist, Ava Mattiske, who is also the face painter at the Ashton Show…"

Crap.

THERE WERE MURMURINGS of recognition. Caleb just stared at the floor. So much for nobody he knew being there. Then Richo elbowed him in the ribs and said loudly, "Hey, isn't that your friend, the one who painted you as Peppa Pig?"

Chuckles rang out. Someone guffawed.

"Yeah, thanks for remembering that little detail, Richo." But who wouldn't remember, when the evidence was still stuck up on the noticeboard in the kitchen for all to see?

"Settle down, Peppa, settle down," Mike continued with a smirk. "Anyhow, it turns out Ava's having a big exhibition of her works in EJ's Gallery and Café, and EJ's had a word in her ear about how we came to his rescue the other month when his kitchen caught fire and so she's kindly agreed to donate ten per cent of the proceeds from her artwork sales to the Burns Unit at the local Children's Hospital. So I've told the gallery owner that we'll turn out to rattle a few tins and support a local artist and this worthy cause, and he's agreed to match the funds raised dollar for dollar. And so if you fancy buying yourself a painting to hang on a wall, I won't go stopping you. Okay, so I need four volunteers…"

Caleb sighed. God, what were the bloody chances? "I'm in," he called from the back, shoving up his hand.

Mike looked at him and frowned, checking something on his clipboard. "I thought you took yourself off the on call list for tomorrow night."

Caleb nodded. "Yeah, but I figure this'll only go for a couple of hours and it's for such a great cause." Like keeping his identity secret for a start. He didn't want anyone knowing he was the one in those pictures, and if he wasn't on that roster and his mates turned up and found him out of uniform alongside Ava, that was going to look mighty suspicious. And he wasn't going to not turn up at all, just to avoid being seen. Not when he plans for afterwards.

"Okay," Mike said, putting down his name. "Who else?"

Tina put up her hand, swiftly followed by Matt, the rookie, and Caleb wondered if there wasn't some young love going on down there.

"Anyone else?" Mike said, scanning the group.

"Aw, hell," Richo said. "Put me down."

"Excellent," said Mike. "Thanks, all. Okay, back to work."

Caleb turned to Richo, horrified that the one guy in the crew who knew him best, the one he spent the most time with in the gym and the one who had the best chance of recognising him in Ava's paintings, even if headless, was going to be there. "You, donating your time for a worthy cause on a Friday night when you could be at the pub? What's come over you?"

Richo shrugged. "Yeah, I thought the same thing at first, but I've never been to an art gallery. I reckon it might be a good way to meet some new chicks."

Caleb just shook his head and headed back to the showers.

Great. Just great. Three guys from his station there on the opening night, with not one but four pictures of his naked body on display. Okay, so torso, rather than body. But Ava better have been right about nobody being able to tell who it was.

Now he was really sweating.

CALEB LEFT THE station after his shower, heading for a catch up with Dylan down at the Maylands Hotel, felt the sting of the sun in the sky and instinctively looked up at the hills, thinking of Ava, alone in her little stone cottage perched overlooking the Uriarra Gorge.

Summer was really turning up the heat, with no signs of relenting any time soon. The forecast looked ominous, with talk of catastrophic conditions looming across several areas of Southern Australia, and everyone at the station, it seemed, had one eye permanently checking the range of hills that bordered one side of Adelaide, simultaneously fearing the worst while hoping for the best.

In nineteen eighty-three, two years before Caleb and Dylan had been born, fire had ravaged the Adelaide Hills, in what had become known as the Ash Wednesday bushfire. Twenty-eight people had died that February day. There'd been other fires since then too, Cherryville in 2013 and

Sampson Flat in 2015, and they'd caused plenty of grief and loss of property too. But in in the back of everyone's mind loomed the memories of the Black Saturday bushfires in Victoria in 2009 where 173 people had perished, and the fact that since Ash Wednesday, there were more than two thousand new homes built by tree changers wanting to live in the Adelaide Hills amongst the bush that made it such a beautiful place to live, and that it was a disaster waiting to happen.

Because one day, it would burn again.

He chewed his lip, thinking of her up there alone if the worst happened, glad he'd checked the diesel pump the other day but knowing that the sprinkler system he'd had her install and even the little retreat room behind her studio were sensible precautions but by no means silver bullets. When you were faced with monstrous bushfires, nobody was going to give a guarantee, whatever precautions you took. He'd talk to her about her bushfire plan, make sure she was getting right out of there if the forecast predicted catastrophic conditions. He didn't want her taking any chances. Not with her life.

CALEB AND THE crew had a call out to a brush fence fire the next day, that, in the stinking hot and windy conditions, had quickly spread into an overhanging roadside tree and the two cars parked underneath it. By the time the first appliance arrived, the fence, trees, and cars were well alight and a carport attached to the house was in danger. To the pistol shots of car windscreen and side windows exploding, the crew got out the hoses and set to drenching the burning cars and fence, and towing a third car clear before it too could catch alight.

"That's the third brush fire in the eastern suburbs in as many days," said Richo when the flames had been doused and they were rolling up the hoses. "Reckon we've got ourselves a firebug on the loose."

Caleb nodded. These kinds of fires always seemed to come in spates, made all the more worrying by idiots inspired to carry out similar copycat attacks. "I think our police buddies agree with you, too." They were already on the case, interviewing the neighbours to seek out witnesses and, best of all, any neighbourhood security videos.

"Dylan's crew got called out to one the other day. He reckons—"

"Hey," Caleb interrupted, slamming the hose door, "when were you talking to Dylan?" He'd had drinks with his brother just last night and he hadn't mentioned anything about having deep and meaningful conversations with any of his crew mates. The thought was decidedly discomforting. It was bad enough Richo had his phone number.

"Hey, don't get touchy. He might be your brother, but he is allowed to talk to other people."

"Yeah? Well, what else did you talk about? You didn't

call him up to talk about brush fence fires, I take it."

"I didn't call him up," he huffed. "I dropped by my old station for farewell cake because one of the guys in my old crew was leaving and Dylan happened to be there. Is that allowed, Peppa?"

"Don't call me that."

"Sorry, forgot, should have said Peppa Pig. Won't make that mistake again."

Caleb rolled his eyes. "You're an idiot, Richo."

He snorted. "I know. That's why you love me."

If Caleb didn't know his life couldn't be in safer hands with Richo at his back, he'd almost think him a drongo, but Caleb knew how good his crew mate was on the job and that he just liked to come across as the clown. Every crew had to have one.

He shook his head. "Dylan's welcome to you. Come on," he said, shutting the last equipment door. "Let's blow this joint."

He drove the appliance back to the station, thinking about the conversation with Dylan last night, and got a wave from a busload of school kids they were parked next to at an intersection.

"Turn on your siren!" yelled one boy, standing at a window looking bug-eyed at them. Caleb flicked on the flashing lights for a second to give the kid a thrill and they waved as the lights turned green and they took off, and Caleb got back to the serious business of chewing over that convo with

Dylan again.

Dylan hadn't mentioned anything about talking to Richo, true, but then he had been a tad distracted. Dylan must have checked his phone at least a dozen times. Boy, he had it bad for this Hannie chick. Although Caleb would bet the sex was nowhere near as good as what he and Ava shared. Talk about combustible.

Not that he could tell anyone.

The sex was as great as ever – bloody brilliant, in fact – and Ava had welcomed him back to her bed, but it was almost like their conversation the night of the Ashton Show had never happened. If he'd thought she'd loosen up, he'd been wrong. Instead, she'd gone back to being the way she'd always been, expecting him to fall in likewise.

And that wasn't what he'd signed back on for. And while he didn't know what was holding her back, he sensed it was yielding, that he was even back in the picture at all. And it was time to press her again.

And one day soon he might even get to take her out to the local pub for dinner, instead of eating in or getting in takeaway, so that nobody saw them out together and put two and two together. One day, they might go visit a winery or three, there were so many good ones he'd heard about in the hills that did tasting platters and wines, and then go to the fancy cheese shop in Hahndorf and buy some cheeses to go with the wine. Like normal people who didn't have to skulk around in the shadows did.

One day, it'd be nice to take her out and show her off and say, yeah, this is my woman.

"Oi! Caleb!"

"What?"

"Where the hell were you? Mars?" Richo said. "It's like trying to talk to a bloody statue."

"I was thinking," he growled. "You ought to try it some time. So what did you want?"

"Just wondering if you wanted to go out for a drink later tonight, after this art thing?"

"It's an exhibition, not a 'thing'."

"Ooh, touchy. So, you want to go out after this"– he put on a hoity toity voice–"'ex-hi-bi-ti-on' then?"

"Nope."

"Why not?"

"Because I've already got plans that don't include you."

"Who do they include?"

He looked over at his crew mate. "None of your damned business."

"So it's a woman then."

Caleb rolled his eyes. "Yeah, it is, actually."

Richo sat up straighter in his seat, clearly thinking he was on a winner and determined to dig deeper. "And do I know her?"

"You do, as a matter of fact. It's Mum," he lied, "*and* she's cooking a lamb roast." At least that bit wasn't exactly a lie, because roast lamb was Dad's favourite and she could well have been.

Richo's eyes narrowed suspiciously. "I'm not really sure I believe you."

Caleb indicated and made sure the station forecourt was clear before he did a bit sweeping arc with the appliance, before then reversing in to the station, and then he turned to his mate, smiled sweetly and said, "I'm not really sure I care."

THE NIGHT WAS as hot as the day, the city stuck in the grip of a heatwave that didn't want to let go, and even at near six pm, the temperature was hovering in the high thirties.

The four fireys uniformed up and travelled to the gallery together in one of the appliances. EJ's Gallery was situated in an old stone building that started life as the local school, the big, high ceilinged rooms and wide corridors lending themselves to all kinds of art installations and exhibitions, although admittedly the only time Caleb had been inside was that time the toaster had caught fire in the kitchen.

For the next month though, Ava's art works were taking pride of place, and he walked in to see the walls hung with her pictures, the colours popping against the neutral backdrop, and Caleb felt a burst of pride. Positioned around her studio, the assembled collection had looked fantastic. Here, skilfully arranged around the gallery walls, the collection was even more stunning, with already a large crowd in attendance, circulating and admiring the works, the number growing by the minute. And all he wanted to do was find Ava and pull her into his arms and tell her how proud of her he was. And, maybe, if tonight went the way he planned, he might be able to.

"Thank god for air conditioning," Richo said beside him, tugging at his collar, and Caleb agreed, the air conditioners thankfully belting out cool air so walking inside had felt like stepping from a furnace to a fridge and they didn't have to feel like dicks in their uniforms when everyone else was wearing short sleeves or strapless cocktail dresses.

As it turned out, he didn't have to look for Ava. She surprised him by finding him. They'd only been there five minutes and she singled him out. "The tap in the kitchen is stuck. You don't think you could give me a hand with that, do you?"

Richo was just about to step forward when Caleb stopped him with a hand to his chest. "That's okay, buddy, I reckon I've got this one covered. You go rattle some tins for charity."

She slipped through a door marked private and he followed right behind, black and white attired waiters carrying trays of canapes or bearing glasses of sparkling wine going the other way. God, but she looked gorgeous tonight. She was wearing a red silk sleeveless blouse over black silk pants and sandals, the material floating about her slim form as she walked, and she'd tied her hair into a knot at the back of her head that he itched to undo later and let her hair sweep down over her bare shoulders after he'd undressed her. Through another door and they were in the kitchen. More people. He cursed the crowd scene, itching as he was right now to pull her into his arms.

Bugger them. He couldn't wait until later. She turned to face him and in the same moment he caught her in his arms and pulled her to him, kissing her hard on her open mouth, letting her know he was here for her, before, just as quickly, letting her go.

She blinked her surprise, her eyes bright. "Wow." Then she gave him a quick once-over. "I've never seen you in uniform before."

"And?"

She looked him up and down again. "I like it," she said, with a smile, "maybe I should draw you with more clothes on next time." She sucked in a quick breath then, as if suddenly remembering why she was here and what was at stake.

He put a hand to her shoulder. He could see the tension around her eyes, she had so much riding on this exhibition, and, while he ached to pull her into his arms and kiss her again and kiss her nerves away, there was a constant stream of foot traffic going in and out behind them. "Are you nervous?"

"A little. It's the biggest solo show I've done." She looked up at him and took a deep breath. "Actually, I'm really nervous."

"You shouldn't be. It looks amazing. It's going to be a huge success. I'm so proud of you, Ava."

She smiled up at him and put a hand to his chest and even through his jacket Caleb felt like she was reaching right inside to his heart. "Thank you for being here. Are you still okay for later?"

He sure was. He had dinner already ordered, a bottle of champagne chilling in the fridge at home, along a bunch of red roses to pick up on the way, and a feeling that he wasn't wrong about this thinking tonight was going to be special.

He lifted her hand, pressing his lips to it. "I'll be there."

The door behind them opened again. "Anyone seen our—Oh, there you are, Ava."

"Evan."

He looked at the watch at his wrist. "We're about to get started with the speeches. Ten minutes, does that sound okay?" He looked over at Caleb, his eyes narrowing and Caleb wondered if he remembered him from the kitchen fire, only to be surprised when he said, "You wouldn't be our life model, would you?"

"Me?" He turned to Ava.

She smiled apologetically. "Evan asked if you'd be here. I told him I was hoping you'd make it."

"A firefighter, eh," Evan said, thrusting out his hand, looking delighted. "That makes a lot of sense. You've got quite the fan club going on out there right now, Mr..."

"Caleb," he said, shaking the other man's hand, not entirely comfortable with the thought of a fan club. "Caleb Knight."

"Good to meet you, Caleb. Now, Ava, we should be—"

"Oh," Caleb interrupted, "and Evan?"

"Yes?"

"I'd just like to point out that nobody's supposed to know that it's me out there. I'd appreciate it if we could keep it that way."

The gallery owner made a display of zipping his lips, before he unzipped them to say, "Your secret's safe with me." And he promptly zipped them up again.

CALEB DID A lap of the rooms trying to look like nothing more than a random firefighter volunteering his time collecting donations, but couldn't help but notice on "that" wall, that there were only three of Ava's pictures of him hanging there. The one featuring his naked butt cheeks was missing. Clearly not suitable for a family show, thank god. He found Richo up the back of the room talking to Tina and Matt about the merits or otherwise of the artworks.

"Not my kind of thing," Richo said, sounding disappointed while he did a three-sixty gesturing towards the artwork. "Pots, fruit and flowers, and then more pots and fruit." He shook his head and pointed to end wall that had been dedicated to Ava's nudes. "And as for the beefcake over there, it'd be a bit gay, if I went for that, don't you reckon?"

"I don't think you'd get a look in anyway," Tina said, "not given the interest from that lot."

Caleb winced at the crowd of women standing in front of pictures of him – admiring Ava's skilful pencil strokes, he told himself, because he couldn't afford to let himself think anything else.

"Didn't you say you came here to meet girls, Richo?" Caleb said. "Nobody thought you were here to buy works of art. What are you doing standing up the back?"

His mate sighed and held out his hands. "Dude, here I am, a firefighter decked out in all my firefighting best, and all the women are over there checking out the beefcake. I mean, they buy our Christmas calendars like crack cocaine. I really thought I'd be in with a chance here."

"There, there," Caleb said, patting him on the back, finally starting to relax now that nobody had twigged – in fact, nobody seemed to have the slightest clue – starting to enjoy the evening and feeling prouder than ever of Ava.

"Maybe you should take your shirt off," suggested Tina to Richo. "Give the beefcake a bit of competition."

"I will if you will," Richo said, and Matt, who had up until now been standing alongside Tina and looking equally bored with the exhibition, punched him in the arm with his rattling donations tin. "Maybe you just need a bigger hose."

"Hey," said Richo, looking from Tina to Matt, "what is this? A tag team?"

"Behave," growled Caleb, liking the way Matt was taking

it up to the older man. He wasn't sure if there was something going on between the kid and Tina, but he was fitting in just fine. "They're about to start the speeches."

"Hey," whispered Richo, leaning closer, "how did you get on with that tap?"

"What tap?"

"Phht," he said, nodding knowingly. "I thought as much."

And Caleb, who had rarely been tempted to give an adult a clip around the ear, was sorely tempted now.

Evan was standing behind a lectern ready to introduce Ava by his side – Ava, who was standing all alone, sending Caleb an arrow loaded at the tip with guilt. He should be there to support her, not standing at the back of the crowd like some someone who didn't give a damn. He gave way more than that.

Evan clapped his hands and started his introduction, starting with his thanks to the attendees, and to the great cause this night was supporting through donations to the Children's Hospital Burns Unit by Ava, the caterers and by slashing his own commission, which he made a big point of, and then waited for the applause. Satisfied, he next paid tribute to the firefighters who'd volunteered their time to support the exhibition, firefighters from the station whose quick response had saved the gallery from burning down a few weeks before.

"Damn right," said Richo, puffing up his chest, as the

crowd applauded some more.

He moved on to introducing Ava then, a woman who'd had a childhood dream of being an artist but who'd had to fund her studies painting faces at every Sunday market and fair going, but whose realism set a new benchmark in the art world. An artist who wove her art around the natural world and turned still life into a snapshot of real life.

With every word, Caleb felt his respect for this woman growing. He'd never known of her struggle to fund her way through art school. She'd never told him she'd painted children's faces to pay for her studies. It grieved him that there was still so much about her he didn't know.

"Ladies and gentleman – and our wonderful firefighters who we never thank enough," Evan said, extending his arm to them and garnering an extra round of cheers, "I give you the artist, Ava Mattiske."

Ava's speech was brief, directed to her art and what she'd been trying to achieve – she talked to the theme of the exhibition, of texture and how it enriched all our lives. She talked about the rugged texture of the land where she lived and how it informed her art and how, through her works, she hoped to show there was texture in everything – from the pitted yellow skin of a lemon, to the remarkable skin-scape of the human body – if we only looked closely enough. And we were all the richer for it.

As the applause rose, Caleb's heart swelled. He couldn't remember ever feeling this proud of anyone in his life. He watched on as Evan handed her a huge arrangement of flowers, swapping them with the microphone. "I'm gratified to see the number of red dots already on the paintings on this collection, and seriously thinking you're not charging enough, Ava."

There was a ripple of laughter.

"But, now, for the big event. We've held back on releasing one picture in the collection for sale, because we think the price should be set by the market and so this particular picture is being put up for silent auction and an auction that will run the entire month of the exhibition, so there's plenty of time to come in and take another look and make a bid. And I'm very pleased to say that Ava is donating one hundred percent of the proceeds for this particular picture to the Burns Unit and the Children's Hospital, so I'm hoping that you all dig deep.

"So here it is..."

With the help of an assistant, the covered canvas was raised to a stand on the podium.

Caleb groaned while the audience oohed and aahed, because there, on the podium in the middle of the room where everyone could see it, no matter where they stood, was Caleb, sprawled on the bed, his majestic butt cheeks on full display at head height. He glanced over at Ava, sending her a silent *what the fuck?* But she just shrugged apologetically.

Beside him, Richo was staring. Hard. "Geez, mate," he said with a laugh, "if I didn't know better, I'd reckon that could almost be you."

Caleb's breath stalled in his throat. "Good thing you know better then," he said, when finally he could breathe again, "in that case."

"No, seriously, it does look a bit like you. Look, even the tatt on the arm."

He snorted, never more pleased that he'd begged Ava to blur the lettering of the family motto wherever it appeared. "Everyone's got tatts these days."

His mate peered close. "But—"

"Come on, Richo, you think a woman who sees me as Peppa Pig is going to use me as some life model?"

And Richo looked at him and smirked. "Yeah, dumb ass idea, hey." He pointed to Caleb's face. "Now, *that* was a work of art."

And it was Caleb's greatest pleasure to punch his mate on the arm.

He saw Ava across the room and threaded his way over, rattling his tin for donations on the way, trying to look inconspicuous, but she was way too busy talking to guests sipping wine and talking about her work to talk to him and he made his disconsolate way back. He was seeing her after. It could wait.

Richo was nowhere to be seen when he got back.

"Where did Richo get to?" he asked Tina.

"Over there," she said, gesturing with her tin, "checking out the artwork. I think he might be interested in making a bid."

Caleb turned around and groaned when he saw Richo standing in front of the picture, his mobile phone cocked in front of his face. Good grief. He headed straight over, not making a pretence of stopping for donations this time, and planted himself between the picture and Richo. "What the hell do you think you're doing?"

"Admiring the art work," he said, shifting to one side and clicking off another photo.

"Will you stop that? You're making an idiot of yourself."

Richo pulled the phone from his eyes. "Ahem, *who* exactly is making an idiot of himself? I'm not the one posing for nudey pictures. You really thought I fell for that crap you just spun?"

Caleb looked around, saw several curious heads in a nearby group turned in their direction from which one woman emerged with a notebook in her hand looking from one man to the other. "Excuse me, did I hear you say this man is our model? I'm Valerie Robertson, from *The Eastern Reporter*, do you think we could get a photo of you in front of the painting?"

Richo grinned and cocked his finger at him. "Gotcha," he said, and then to a young woman standing alongside Valerie. "Ava asked me to pose first, but I'm the shy type."

She raised her eyebrows and gave him a quick once-over before she held out one hand. "I'm Gillian," she said with a smile. "It's lovely to meet you. But I'm sure you'd make a fabulous model yourself."

IT WAS JUST on dark when they returned to the station, though the temperature had hardly budged, the air over Adelaide like sitting under a hot blanket. Thankfully, still a smoke free blanket. Caleb got changed and picked up his keys, heading for his car.

Richo was heading out at the same time, clearly in a hurry.

"Where's the fire?"

His mate winked. "I've got a date with Gillian. I reckon I'm in there."

"Lucky Gillian."

"Oh hey," said Richo, with a wink, his keys poised in his hand. "Be sure to say hi to your mum for me. Wink. Wink."

And Caleb was in such a good mood, he even managed a wry smile. The exhibition opening had been an amazing success and there was still a month to run. Sure, he hadn't been too thrilled about the whole bare-assed silent auction thing, but he was beginning to see there might be a bright side to even that. "Sure. I'll do that."

Five minutes later, he had the takeaway collected and the chilled champagne and roses on board and fifteen minutes later he was up high in the hills, the lights of the city twinkling far below. For once, she actually came outside to greet him, like she'd been waiting impatiently for him to get there, her eyes bright as she threw her arms around his neck so ferociously he had to hold his arms out to the sides to protect his precious cargo.

"Can you believe how well tonight went?" And then she took his face in her hands and kissed him so passionately on the mouth, it was a miracle he didn't throw the champagne and roses away and bundle her up in his arms and take her straight to bed.

"You're a star," he told her breathlessly, when he could get a word in between her kisses. "These are for you, in recognition of how brilliant you are."

"Champagne!" she said, clutching the bottle. "And flowers." She smiled up at him, the golden highlights in her eyes incandescent. "This is the best day."

And Caleb knew it was, all the way down to his toes. And, if he had his way, it was about to get even better.

"I'm so sorry about the picture and silent auction thing," she said, as they made their way inside, still wrapped in each other's arms. "It was Evan's idea at the last moment. I hope you don't mind."

He had, at the time, and he'd been even more aghast when Richo had blown his secret wide open, but now he was getting to like the idea of people knowing about their relationship. Once upon a time, it had suited them both to keep it secret, but as far as he was concerned it was way past its use by date. It was time it came out of the closet. "Forget it," he told her. "It's for a good cause."

"You know, the last bid they had tonight was for eighteen hundred dollars?"

"What? You are kidding me?"

"No. And it will go higher while the exhibition runs."

He shook his head as they unpacked takeaway containers. He'd gone all out and bought half a dozen dishes tonight because a celebration deserved a feast, and that was what they had from red duck curry and chilli prawns to the soft shell crab he knew she loved. They sat cross-legged on the rug with the dishes set out on the coffee table between them, glasses of champagne at the ready.

"To you," he said, toasting his clever Ava.

"And to you," she added, "my amazing, accidental life model." She took a sip of her wine and said, "Oh, wait. I've got something for you." And she rose to her feet and moved away with that fluid, silken grace thing that stirred his senses like a physical caress. Moments later, she was back. "This is for you," she said, handing him a twelve-inch square package wrapped in brown paper and tied up with a big white bow.

"It's to thank you for being my inspiration. Even if inadvertently."

"I didn't mind," he said, undoing the bow and pushing the ribbon aside. He'd discovered that being a life model came with benefits, like that skin tingling awareness that someone was watching you. Someone that you were about to get down and dirty with.

He tore the paper away and felt like he'd been sucker-punched. "Wow." It was a painting of the flowers he'd given her from his place, the frangipani with the snow white petals and their yellow centres bold against a black satin backdrop. That was the night after the show, the night he'd thought she'd been going to end it, the night she'd put him on notice to keep things cool. And while the latter gave him pause to wonder about what he wanted to tell her tonight, the former gave him hope. She hadn't ended it, which had to mean something, surely? "You did this for me? Seriously?"

She nodded, then screwed up her nose. "It's not too girly, though, is it? A picture of flowers is probably the last thing you want on your bachelor flat walls. Maybe you could give it to your mother."

"Maybe," he said, the picture propped up in his lap, although he knew he'd never let it go. "It's amazing." He looked over at her. "Like you."

She beamed. "Thank you," she said, as she propped herself up on her knees and reached across the table then, wrapping her arm around him and planting another one of her sizzling kisses on his mouth, her tongue coaxing his to play, until his cock twitched and he damned well near forgot about the food in front of them.

He tried to gather her closer, wanting more of her, when she pushed him away. "Eat first," she said, "and then you can play."

He grinned. She was right, there was celebrating to be done first, and it was a feast of colours and spices and tastes they shared, before they peeled each other's clothes away and turned to feast on each other, this time a sensual, passionate feast for the body and the senses.

"You're really something special, you know," he said, after they'd fallen apart, boneless and breathless, their bodies glistening with sweat on the sheets of her big, wide bed. It was too hot for even a sheet tonight. The curtains were flung apart, windows open, hoping to catch a breeze and letting in the twinkle of the city lights far below, while above them a fan did lazy laps that blew the sluggish night air around.

Their faces scant inches apart, he stroked the pad of his thumb across her lips, the puff of her ragged breathing warm against his flesh.

She kissed his thumb as it made its passes. "Don't say that."

"Why not, when it's the truth? You're amazing, Ava. Talented, beautiful, and caring. You're the whole package."

Against his arm, she squirmed and shook her head. "No."

"You realise our secret is out. Richo twigged. And once that photo of us gets in the paper, everyone's going to know."

"I know." She sighed. "I'm sorry. I didn't want that to happen. I haven't worked out what to do about that yet."

He waited a beat, knowing he was setting something in motion that he didn't know how would end, but he knew she'd had the chance to discard him once before, and she hadn't taken it, and all he could do was try to get through to her. "I'm not sorry."

Her head rolled towards his. "Why? We agreed from the beginning this was our secret."

He watched the rotating blades doing laps above the bed. "I know," he started, but slowly, knowing the very least he was risking ruining this sublime evening between them, and recognising there was much more at stake than that. But there was no going back now, not if they were ever going to move out of this damned rut they were stuck in once again, and finally move forward. "But the way I see it now, we're a bit like that fan up there, spinning around and around, always on the move and yet ultimately going nowhere. Maybe it's good the secret's out. Maybe now we can go out together for a meal or to the movies because we don't have to pretend that there's nothing going on."

He felt her stiffen beside him, warm responsive flesh turning hard and impossibly cold for such a hot summer's night. And even though she was still there, alongside him, he was aware of her shifting away from him, the distance between them growing by the second, and he hated that he was doing this, but this time, he had no choice.

"Like you said, it's been more than a year and, despite the odd bump in the road, we're still together. Doesn't that tell you something, Ava? Doesn't it suggest that maybe it's time to set what we have free from these constraints, to give this thing some oxygen, and to see if it will survive in the real world?"

"Why would we want to do that?"

He closed his eyes. Even her voice, so husky from their recent lovemaking, was edged with cold. Then he opened his eyes and turned his head to hers, her face a play of light and shadow and like her life, he suddenly realised, filled with shadowed depths no light could see into, and he ached to shine a light in and find out what was lurking there. "Because we can. Because we don't have to hide it from the world any longer because soon the whole damned world is going to know. But, most of all, because it's time."

She sat up, reached for her blue robe and slipped it over her arms. "You know what we agreed, right? You remember?"

"I remember. I also remember you walking out when I told you I wanted more. I never thought I'd see you again, but here I am. Why do you think you let me back in?"

"Because of the exhibition. Because you had such a part in that."

He reached over and put his hand over hers where they lay in her lap. She didn't shy away from his touch, but neither did she make any effort to turn her hand and lace her fingers in his. "You honestly think that's all it was?

She scoffed, rising from the bed and crossing to the window, her hands clutching her arms, her outline illuminated in the glow from the city. "You're kidding yourself, you know that?"

He raised himself up onto one elbow. "No, I think you're the one doing that. I think you're a fake."

Her head spun around. "What did you say? This coming from the person who was, not two minute ago, telling me how amazing I was supposed to be?"

He rolled himself higher on the bed. "And I still think you're amazing, on so many levels, and I'm still so proud of you. But I get this impression you like to make out you're made of Teflon, and that you can glide through your life and the people you meet, and nothing and nobody sticks. I think you like to believe I don't feel anything for you and you like to pretend that you feel nothing for me, and maybe in the beginning that was true for both of us, but I don't believe it now. Because I do care about you, and I keep getting this feeling, that you care for me, more than what you want to let on."

"Why are you doing this?" She put her hands over her face. "You're risking everything!"

He snorted. "But that's just it, Ava. What is this everything we're supposed to be having? We skulk around having furtive rendezvous and secret sex. While the rest of the time we go around pretending we're strangers who mean nothing to each other. Don't you see? When it all comes down to it, we have nothing. So the answer to your question has to be, yes, I am willing to risk what little we have for the chance of a proper relationship. A normal relationship. With you and me and no more secrets, and we'll see where it takes us."

"It will take us nowhere!"

"That may well be true. But what if it's not? What are we throwing away by closing our eyes and not even looking? We could be together. Maybe make a family together. Have children."

She looked aghast. "I told you from the very beginning that I wasn't looking for a relationship. You said all you wanted was sex. They were your words, your terms, and all I did was agree with you! And now you want to change things you dare to tell me I'm fake?"

"Why do you keep going back to that? That was twelve months ago, an entire year. Are you the same person you were back then? Because I'm sure not. I've had twelve months of being with you and getting to know you and, yes, having some of the best sex I've ever had, and what I've learned from that, is that the more I'm with you, the more I want to be with you. And not just for the sex and not in brief snatches of time. Not in secret. Jeezus, Ava, now that it's going to be out in the open, can't we at least give a normal relationship a try?"

And in the glow from the city lights, he could see her downturned lips and her sorrowful eyes. "I knew I should have ended it."

His gut jerked but he wasn't about to give in. "You had the chance, but you didn't, did you? And why was that, did you ever stop to think, unless you didn't really want it to end? You care for me, I know you do. Just like I care for you. I just don't understand why you can't admit it. Why are we insisting that we mean nothing to each other, when, from what I can tell, each other is the one thing we both cling to? When each other is all we have?"

She stood against the window, unmoving, unrelenting, and as still and cold as a statue. A column of blue ice impervious to the smothering heat.

"I think you should go now."

"I'll go," he said, gathering up his scattered clothes, knowing he'd said all he'd wanted to say, hoping she wasn't as impervious to his words, "but only to give you time to think. And this time I really want you to think, Ava, about what we could be together, instead of this pathetic little half-life we've been squeezing ourselves into until now." He pulled on his shorts, not bothering with his underwear, and snatched up his few remaining items. "And I'm not going to wait this time. I'm not going to hang around waiting for you to see sense. I'll be back tomorrow for your answer," he said, not making a move towards her when he knew that was the last thing she wanted. "I'll talk to you then."

AVA STOOD UNDER the shower for a long time after Caleb had gone, letting the water stream over her head and body, wanting it to wash away this sense of emptiness and utter desolation, willing anger to fill the void. Why did he have to make it so complicated? It had started out easy enough, the boundaries clear, finding pleasure in each other's bodies and as well as enjoying an easy rapport that had been fun – for a while. But lately, just lately, things had started to go wrong.

She wanted to turn the clock back and return to those simpler times.

But now he was talking about becoming a family. Having children. Dear god, what kind of mother would she be? What kind of parent *could* she be after the parents she'd had? After what they'd turned her into, her bed a revolving door for her father's business cronies?

The water rained down on her and she let it run, for once casting off all thought of conserving the water in her rainwater tanks. There was rain forecast for the coming week and tonight she needed the touch of something against her flesh that might wash away the bleakness of her soul.

She slapped her open hand against the tiled wall, embracing the sting, searching for anger. She wanted to be angry, not to feel this deep sense of loss.

Why couldn't he have listened to her? Why had he had to go and make things so complicated?

She leaned her forehead against the wall and let the water course down her spine, knowing Caleb wasn't the one she should be angry with.

Because wasn't this the way it always ended?

And she knew, she damned well knew in her heart, that she'd been a fool. She should never have trusted him to keep his end of the deal.

Not when there was nobody she could trust.

Chapter Eight

CALEB WOKE TO the news of a fire that had broken out overnight in the Adelaide Hills, and his heart slammed into his chest, his first thoughts for Ava. He tried to call her, only to have her phone go straight to message bank. Every time he tried it went straight to message bank, and finally he left one telling her to turn on her radio and listen for updates or better still, get out now.

He headed to the station consumed with guilt. If he'd still been at her place this morning – if he hadn't gone home – if he'd left his bloody I-care-about-you speech for another time, a later time, he would have brought her down to the city with him, even if kicking and screaming. He wouldn't have let her stay up there. He would have given her the keys to his unit. Then whatever happened, he would at least have known she was safe.

The station was buzzing. Every available firey had been called in for what they had been dreading all summer long. And every single one of them knew the monster they could be facing and what was at stake. In no time from those first reports, from the city and suburbs, it looked like the entire range was alight, palls of thick grey smoke rising like massive clouds.

He'd grown up in the Adelaide Hills. Half the people he'd gone to school with still lived there. The house he'd grown up in at Reynolds Ridge, the little stone school house where he and his brother and their friends had gone to school, the scout hall where he'd stuck a fork through his foot planting tomatoes, all of it under threat.

Along with Ava. He'd left her alone up there – was she still there? – and with a fire breaking out and already burning on so many fronts, god only knew where the fire would break out next.

His crew screamed out of the station, lights flashing, heading to a tiny hamlet in the direct path of the flames to help out the local CFS crews who had radioed for assistance. There was no time for regrets then, no time for guilt, when one hundred percent of his energies was required to focus on the job. Working with the local CFS crew and pumping water out of a backyard swimming pool, they managed to push the flames back from one house while the house next door couldn't be saved and was razed to the ground. They came upon two dogs tied up outside another home, tying themselves in knots as they reared in panic, howling in fear as the roaring firestorm approached, and managed to cut them loose them before a fireball leapt from the tree tops and flames engulfed that house too. They found a woman in tears running along the road, her car and trailer broken down, desperate to get to her beloved horses and begging them to save them, when they'd just come from that direction and knew it was futile and there was no hope for any poor animal caught up in that, and they snatched her, weeping in despair, to safety too.

Time after time, they battled the flames and sometimes they won, but sometimes they were beaten back and had to retreat and just let the fire have its head and try to attack it from a different angle.

But when finally, exhausted, they stopped in at the local sports club taken over for feeding and watering the emergency workers, Caleb had time to pay heed to the roiling feeling in his gut. His phone proved useless, telephone towers down, communication limited to radio contact. Even learning that Dylan was up there in Uraidla at Fire Command Centre was no damned good to him when he couldn't get a bloody signal to ask him for updates.

All he knew was that, like the sick feeling in his gut, the fire was growing.

Watered and fed, they were sent back out to the fire ground, working side by side their fellow crews and the water tankers to try to get a handle on this massive roaring beast.

At night they battled on, the clouds glowed red from the fire dancing over the range and looking like the very gates of hell.

And, as one day rolled into the next, the fire relentless in its hunger, devouring everything in its path, it was nothing to the hell he felt inside.

Where was Ava?

In the end, it was two days he hadn't been able to contact her. Two days of fires raging out of control and taking out phone towers and huge trees falling and blocking roads and not knowing whether she was still at her home or evacuated and holed up somewhere.

Two days of hoping and praying that if she was still home, that the fire didn't make it into the Uriarra Gorge or there'd be no stopping it.

Two fucking days and nights of not knowing and he had never felt more powerless in his life.

But there was one thing Caleb did know. That he'd been wrong that night, to tell Ava that he cared for her, wrong to let her think that was all it was.

Because you didn't feel like a part of you would die if anything happened to someone you merely cared about. You wouldn't feel like you had lost everything there was to lose.

No, this thing he felt for her had grown bigger than that. And when he finally managed to track Ava down, he was going to damn well tell her.

The promised rains arrived on the morning of the third day, delivering relief to weary firefighters on the fire ground and terrified residents who'd been in the path of the fire alike, but there was still no rest for Caleb and his crew, no rest for any crews, the smoking fire ground needing to be monitored while roads had to be cleared of fallen trees while still others deemed unsafe needed to be cut down.

He got a message via radio that their old home in the hills had escaped the flames, while others around it had been razed, and, for that, he gave silent thanks, but still his phone was useless to him, and it was only the map of the fire ground at the sports ground that gave him comfort. The bushfire had cut a great swathe through the hills, but there, on the western fringe, the fire had passed it by. The gorge was safe and Caleb could breathe again.

Now he just had to find Ava.

IT WASN'T UNTIL the next morning that he finally got his chance. He drove up into the hills, still smoking in some places, seeing the devastation the bushfire had wreaked in this part of the hills first hand. Either side of the roads with nothing left but the blackened trunks of trees, gnarled fingers poking into the sky. And all around was the smell of ash and death. A roadblock stopped him in one place – only residents allowed in, and even his day job didn't give him a free pass, there were serious fears of looters, so he didn't push it– and he had to backtrack down to the city and find another way around. But this route was better, the burned footprint of the fire a narrower band and soon that was behind him. He drove higher up the escarpment, the vegetation eerily unscathed here, like some miracle had protected it from the monster the fire had become.

He began to breathe easier then, finally accepting that the maps hadn't lied and that the gorge and the houses that dotted its upper reaches had survived. Most of all that Ava was okay.

He pulled into her driveway, giving thanks for whatever miracle had saved the gorge, his footsteps crunching on the gravel Overhead in a cloudless blue sky, the sun shone, the volume dialled back to autumn while the bush looked refreshed after its drenching. A perfect day to live in the Adelaide Hills, if you still had your home.

He found her tending the small herb garden filled with the coriander and Thai basil and mint she used in her cooking that she kept outside the kitchen. Dressed in a singlet over cute bobble fringed shorts that showed off the long satin length of her legs, she'd heard his footsteps and was poised waiting, watering can in one hand, to see who was coming, and after days and nights of not knowing, the urge to run to her and sweep her into his arms and hold her to satisfy himself she was real and he wasn't just imagining her was almost overwhelming.

"Oh, it's you," she said, turning back to her herbs, her cold greeting like a bucket of water to his face.

He crossed the paved patio to her, his heart leaden, but he wasn't going away and he wasn't giving up. He'd never for one moment imagined this was going to be easy.

"Ava," he said, drawing alongside, talking to her downturned profile as she tended her plants.

He ached to reach out a hand to her back, where the thick knot of her hair rested against her back, ached to run his fingers down the sweet curve of her spine, but there was an aura around her, a force field that repelled him and told him not to touch.

"I tried to call."

"I had my phone off."

"I've been worried sick."

This time she turned, the lights in her brandy coloured eyes all but snuffed out, her lips tightly drawn. Did he only imagine their quiver or the tiny tic in the corner of her mouth?

"Why?"

"Why do you think? There were bushfires raging all through the hills and I didn't have a clue what was happening around here or where you were or how you were managing. I was scared witless when I couldn't contact you. I've never been more scared in my life."

She shrugged and turned back to her plants, shifting sideways away from him along the small raised bed, putting down her watering can and picking up some snips, trimming bits here and there. "As you can see, I'm fine. I had my bushfire plan ready, in case things got hairy."

In case things got hairy? "Who are you trying to kid, Ava? This was a major bushfire. If it had got into the gorge, there would have been no stopping it."

"It didn't get into the gorge."

"And that was all kinds of miracle. All it needed was one live ember to land and the whole lot would have gone up, and taken you with it." He raked one hand through his short hair, thinking of the dead livestock in the burnt paddocks and the kangaroos blundering in panic through the burning bush. The horses they found when they could go back... "The things I saw – things you never want to see."

Her eyes snapped up to his, a glimmer of light illuminating their cognac depths. "You were there?"

"Every available firefighter available was there."

She dropped her gaze, turned her face away again.

"Don't you understand? All the time I was seeing what the fire could do, the way it was eating up the bush, I couldn't call you. I didn't know where you were or how you were. I was beyond terrified– I was shit scared."

She put down her snips and brushed her hands. "I can't help that. I'm not responsible for how you feel."

"Maybe not. But you're the reason I feel. I told you I'd give you time to think. I told you I'd be back and here I am."

She shook her head and started back toward the house. "Look, if you're planning on replaying the conversation from that night, I'm afraid going to have to pass. I'm not interested."

He caught one of her hands and spun her, catching her other hand so they faced each other, his thumbs drinking in the satin texture of her skin while making circles on the backs of her trembling hands. He gazed down at her beautiful face with the frightened eyes, feeling the weight of the future bearing down him, and knowing he had to do this right.

"No, not the same conversation. This one is a different one. A far more important one. Because while I was stuck out there fighting this bushfire, with no idea what was happening here or what you were facing, all I knew was that if the worst happened, I could lose you forever. And it tripped a switch in my brain, and made me realise what you really mean to me."

Her eyes filled with panic, and she pulled her hands from his and spun away, crossing her arms across her chest, protecting herself that way she did.

"I don't have to listen to this."

"No, you need to hear this. I don't just care for you, Ava. I love you."

"No!" she cried, flinching as if he'd physically struck her. "No!"

"I love you, Ava," he repeated, because the words sounded so right and she needed to hear it, needed to know what she meant to him. "And I want to spend the rest of my life loving you. I want yours to be the face I see when I go to sleep. I want yours to be the face I wake up to every morning. And I've been walking on eggshells around you, afraid to lose what we have for fear of speaking up, when I realised I could have lost you and never have told you what I now know." He reached a hand to her shoulder, and turned her too him, his eyes imploring. "I love you."

She shook her head, not meeting his eyes. "I don't want your love. I don't want anyone to love me."

"That's something I can't help you with. I can't turn off what I feel for you. I can't stop loving you. And be honest, can you say you don't care about me? You don't feel something for me? You weren't worried the tiniest bit when you realised I'd been up there, fighting that bushfire?"

She looked up at him then, her face a mask filled with shock and horror and fear. "No…'

"I don't believe you."

"You don't understand," she said, her whole body shaking, her eyes wild. "I can't do this. I can't let you love me. I can't let anyone love me. I can't risk it."

"Why?" he demanded. "What's stopping you?"

"Because I know what love leads to!" she cried. "I know how it ends. Because it hurts too much to be broken and I don't want to ever be broken again."

And before his eyes, she seemed to crumple in on herself until she sagged, boneless, to the floor. He scooped her up before she hit the ground, collecting the puddle of flesh and bones she'd become and cradling her close against his chest, wanting to protect her from the pain of what was hurting her.

"Oh, Ava, what happened to you? Who did this to you?"

He pressed his lips to her hair and carried her to her

room, laying her on her bed and holding her close as the sobs racked her body, her keening cries piercing his soul.

And, with every savage convulsion, his anger built. "I love you," he whispered to her, even as she shook her head and told him he mustn't. Yet still she clung to him while the storm moved through her, and still he held her tight, until her shudders subsided and her tears abated, the only sound her fractured gasping breaths.

"What kind of man could do this to you?" he asked her, stroking her hair, because he knew it must have been a man to hurt her so deeply, to make her so afraid of giving too much to another. Gently he lifted her chin to face him, her tear clumped lashes forming spikes around her wounded eyes. "I want to tear whoever did this to you apart."

She sniffled and pushed herself away from him then, curling herself up to sitting on the bed, one arm wrapped around her knees and the other hand swiping at the moisture on her cheeks while she started blindly ahead. "That would be a pointless exercise," she whispered, her voice now eerily calm. "My parents are already dead."

Chapter Nine

S HE HEARD HIS gasp of shock, and knew his mind was joining the dots.

"Oh, Ava," he said, reaching out a hand to her cheek and she saw the look of abhorrence in his eyes, but the confusion too, at what he was hearing. "Is that why…"

His fingertips brushed against her damp skin, and she closed her eyes against the sensation, leaning into it and savouring it, knowing it would be one of the last times they touched.

"I had an idyllic childhood," she started, blinking her eyes open again.

She'd never told anyone about her past before, but she now knew this man would never give up, and it was the only way to make him understand why loving her was futile.

"I couldn't have dreamed for a better one. My mother was an Australian model who worked all over the world for the best houses, Chanel, Valentino, Yves St. Laurent – you name it, she was there strutting the catwalk – when she met my father. He was handsome and magnetic, already a rich man with interests worth countless millions in property development, hotels, and retail."

She flicked the bobbles on her shorts, focusing on something meaningless, inane, while she spilled the toxic details of her life. "They met one evening, at a fashion event in Singapore, and that night he proposed. She gave up her career to become his wife. They were the golden couple, the successful businessman and his supermodel wife. She had golden wavy hair and emerald green eyes, and so glamorous, that as a child, I thought she was the most beautiful woman in the world.

"I grew up thinking it was a fairy tale marriage. And why wouldn't I? I lived in a fairy tale palace for a home, with a fairy tale mother and a fairy tale father, and I was the little princess. That's what my father called me, inviting me into his business meetings from the time I could twirl and be shown off, while all the time my mother dressed me in the prettiest of clothes and then, as a teenager, taught me all the tricks she'd learned as a model, so that one day, I might look as beautiful as her. I knew I never could, because she was so fair, but my mother insisted I try my best. Men liked women to look beautiful, she told me. Men liked women who knew how to look after them."

She paused, temporarily abandoning the bobbles, thinking how naïve she'd been, how she'd loved them and how she'd believed they'd loved her. So she'd trusted them, when all those years they'd been grooming her.

"When I turned sixteen," she said, her throat constricting at the memories, "I was so excited. My father had promised me a surprise for my birthday. He called me into his office late that evening. There was a man there who I knew, the father of a good school friend, and he wished me a happy birthday. He acted strangely when I asked about my friend, but I just thought he was embarrassed he hadn't thought to bring her.

And then my father offered me champagne for the first time – I was sixteen, my father said, and it was time to take my place in the family business – and the men drank a toast to me and I felt so mature and grown up. And then he told me the men had business to do, and called for the brandy as he sent me away.

"I didn't understand what was happening. Not then. Not until later, when my mother took me to a beautiful bedroom in the house I'd never seen before, and on the coverlet of the bed was lingerie all set out, beautiful white silk lingerie my mother told me was a birthday gift, and that I should put on, and get into bed, and wait for my surprise. And even then, I was confused and none of it made any sense, but this was my mother, my beautiful fairy tale mother, and she loved me, and so I trusted her…'

So naïve! She squeezed her eyes shut and rolled her lips between her teeth and bit down.

"You don't have to do this," Caleb growled, his big hand between her shoulders, his fingers trying to stroke comfort into her soul.

"But I do," she bit out without turning. "You have to know. You have to understand why." She took one breath and then another, steadying herself. "Eventually I fell asleep, only to be awakened when I realised there was somebody in the bed with me, a man who reeked of brandy and who was fumbling for me. I screamed, thinking he must have stumbled into the wrong room, the wrong bed, but then he hit me and told me to shut up, and I recognised it was my friend's father and I screamed again. I was so frightened."

She squeezed her eyes shut, cast back to that moment, to that innocent girl whose life was about to be shattered.

"And this time after he hit me, he had the pleasure of telling me, he had paid my father handsomely for the privilege of deflowering his daughter and I should cooperate and enjoy it." She put a hand over her heart, her breathing ragged and rushed until she calmed it, several breaths later.

"That was the first time my father used me as part of his deal making. That was the first time I was expected to take my place in the family business."

She turned her head up to the ceiling, remembering the helplessness she'd felt back then. The fear. The pain. The agony of knowing her fairy tale life had been a lie.

"Christ, Ava...' Beside her Caleb searched for words, but she knew there were none.

This was no flesh wound he could stitch up or stick on a dressing and let it heal. This was betrayal that cut soul deep and there were no dressings, no sutures for that.

"How could they do that to you? How could your mother…"

Ava clutched her arms, trying to laugh then but the sound came out fractured and broken. "I appealed to her, of course. I couldn't believe she knew. I thought she would help. And I remember she held me like when I'd been a child, rocking me, and as she wiped the moisture from my eyes she told me that tears make eyes puffy and that men like their women to look happy and beautiful. And when I told her I didn't understand, she smiled down at me and told me that this was the price for my fairy tale existence. That for twenty years she had been my father's whore, and that it was my turn now."

"Ava." He made to scoop her into his arms then, but she pushed them away and rose from the bed, feeling strangely stronger, as if saying the words out loud had released some of the pressure.

No longer was it her big dark secret. It was out there, in the open, the whole sordid horror of her former existence. She stood by the window, staring out but unseeing, her mind stuck in the past, replaying the video from those former days.

"After that, my home became my prison, palatial and luxurious, but still a prison. I had bodyguards to accompany me when I was allowed out, delivered to hotels or private houses for a rendezvous or a party, but they weren't there to protect me. They were there to ensure I didn't escape."

"God, Ava, I don't know what to say."

"It's okay," she said. "You don't have to say anything." All he had to do was listen and understand, and let her go.

As he would once he knew, knowing any sympathy he had for her would evaporate faster than a spray of mist into the summer air.

"But do you know the worst thing, the very worst thing?"

He shook his head and she smiled. "I enjoyed it." She chewed on the words like they were meat. "I enjoyed the sex. I got good at it. I enjoyed making men come for me and I took pleasure from them any way I could. I wasn't just a good whore. I was the best. I made my father a lot of money."

She shrugged, her jaw clenched, her eyes following the flight of a dozen sulphur crested cockatoos across the sky rather than meet his disappointed eyes rethinking his earlier declaration. Rethinking that she could ever be a mother for his children.

"What changed?" he asked, and she was surprised he hadn't already fled in disgust. "How did you get away?"

"I ran into my old school friend at one of those parties, and she asked what I was doing now and why she never heard from me anymore. But how do you tell someone what their father has done when you know that her parents are still together? When you know her own fairy tale life would unravel or that she would brand you a liar and hate you forever? So what could I tell her other than what I did? That I worked for the family business.

She dropped her head. "And then she asked if I was still painting, because it had been my dream in school, to be a painter one day." She turned her eyes up to his. "I'd forgotten my own dream. And it reawakened something in me, a yearning to be free, to live life the way I wanted.

"By then, my father had grown complacent. I think he believed he had me where he wanted and that I had accepted my fate like my mother had and that I was resigned to exchanging sex for a life of luxury, and being traded like a commodity. And then a chance came up. He sent me to Hong Kong to entertain a man he could potentially make millions from." She looked at Caleb. "My father didn't know I had seduced my bodyguard. He didn't know that I had learned to use the tricks I had been taught against him. I pretended to be happy that we were away together, and he was happy to have me away from my fortress of a house. We had champagne and sex and when he fell asleep, I grabbed my passport and ran. That poor man. I often wonder at the punishment he must have received for letting me slip free." She trailed off and turned to the window.

He must have sensed her guilt and her shame, because he jumped from the bed and caught her chin in his hand and forced her gaze to his. "Ava, you have nothing to feel guilty for. You were fighting for your own freedom. Your own existence."

"I know." She hesitated, her lip between her teeth. "Anyway, I fled straight to the airport. And straight to somewhere I thought was free, where I could hide. I flew to Melbourne. Moved to Sydney. I changed my name to Mattiske. I started a tentative new life as an artist." She took a breath. "I need tea." She ducked around him, heading for the kitchen.

"Is that when you got your tattoo?" he asked, behind her.

She snapped on the kettle smiling at the memory. "Yes. In a dingy tattoo parlour in Kings Cross. I was celebrating my escape. I thought I was free. And I was, although that didn't stop me making bad choices." She pushed her hair behind her ears. "I told you about my agent not working out?"

"Yeah."

She nodded, thinking about Rene and all his promises. "Rene came into a café where I had some pictures for sale. He told me he was an agent and that he would make me a star.

"And for a while it was good. He got me into galleries. He sold my work. And at night he told me he loved me. But I never saw any money. It was always coming, he said, always clearing in a trust account. It never came. And in the end I discovered he had a wife and three children tucked away in western Sydney.

"Tea or coffee?"

"Ava—"

"No, you're right, I guess you won't be staying," she said, putting a teabag for herself in a mug and filling it with the boiled water. "Talk about lurching from one disaster to the next." She turned to face him, leaning against the counter. "But if it taught me something, it's that I had to stand on my own two feet. You accused me of being made of Teflon, that I don't let anything or anyone stick, and I guess that's true. But that's the way I have to be. I have to protect myself because there is nobody else to protect me."

"I would protect you."

"You say that now. But what I learned is that you can't trust anyone, even the people you love, and the people who tell you they love you. That I can't afford to trust anyone other than myself."

"Not everyone who says they love you is out to hurt you, Ava. You have to believe that. I wouldn't hurt you."

"And how can I believe you won't turn on me too? How can I believe you will be there for me, when I need it most? How can I trust you, when I can't trust anyone? I'm broken, Caleb. I've picked myself up and put myself back together twice now, but the joins are still there. I can't afford for that to happen again. I can't go through that again."

She watched him pacing the floor, running his hands through his hair, watched his beautiful self wrestling with finding a way to get through to her, knowing it was futile, and there was none.

He stopped and turned to her, his eyes pleading. "I'm

not like those others, Ava. How do I prove it to you? How can I make you believe me?"

"That's just it," she said. "You can't. I'm sorry, Caleb. This is why we can't be together. This is why it has to end."

Chapter Ten

S HE'D GOT WHAT she wanted. Caleb had laid his cards on the table, each and every one of them, and she'd thrown not only the deck, but the table in his face. That was the risk he'd taken.

He'd known the odds and he'd accepted them.

It was done.

But it didn't mean he had to like it. He hated it. Each and every bit of it. He hated that she had suffered so much at the hands of her own parents. He hated that she had been taken advantage of when she had so desperately needed reassurance and love and the chance to rebuild her shattered life.

No wonder she was so self-protective, betrayed first by the people who should have loved her the most, and then by an agent who'd cheated and lied to her. No wonder she set boundaries and made rules.

But he hated that she couldn't see that he would never hurt her.

Restlessly, Caleb paced the confines of his flat. It didn't

take long to do a lap. There weren't that many rooms and there wasn't a hell of a lot to see. He stopped in the spare room and looked over his collection of bikes. He should take one of them and go for a spin. Later. He stopped in his bedroom, but all he could see was the bed and all he could think about was Ava, and the fact she'd never lie in it again and felt a physical pang that he'd never get to make love to her again. He ended up back in the lounge room but all he could see was that damned picture she'd given him that he'd propped up on the shelf. Of the frangipani flowers he'd given her, their petals bright and bold.

He picked it up and thought about the woman who had painted them. Ava, just as bold and beautiful as those perfect flowers.

And, ultimately, just as fragile.

His phone buzzed from the kitchen where he'd left it charging and for the moment it took him to sweep it up in his hand, he thought that maybe…

But it was Dylan. They hadn't talked since before the bushfire, since that night at the Maylands. Barely a week but it felt like an aeon ago. He picked up, his brain mentally changing gears so he wouldn't sound as hangdog as he felt.

"You sly, bloody dog."

Caleb dragged in a lungful of air and pinched the bridge of his nose. Hard. Clearly his brother wasn't ringing to compare notes about the bushfire. But he supposed this had to come sometime. "Well, hello to you too, Dylan. How're they hanging?"

"Forget my bits, bro. You let me bang on about Hannie the other night, and all this time you never let on."

"About what?"

"I didn't believe it you know. Richo sent me this daft picture—"

Caleb turned to the magnetic *"To Do"* list on his fridge. Scrubbed off milk in number one place and wrote *"Kill Richo!"*

"B—but I didn't believe it could be you, not in a million years."

"Good thinking. You know what Richo's like. Always making something out of nothing."

"Nice try and I might have believed you once upon a time. Before I saw the story in the local paper today. The one with the heading, *Firefighter Bares All for Charity*".

Jeezus! In the pressure cooker conditions of the last few days, he'd forgotten completely about the photo. After the blow up with Ava, it hadn't seemed important any more. "Actually, no," Caleb said, feeling tension building in his head. "I must have missed that."

"You ought to get yourself a copy. It's a keeper. Although I would have called it, Firefighter Bares *Ass* for Charity."

"Ha-ha."

"And don't fret, I'll be sure to pick one up for the folks just in case you forget to get one for Mum's scrapbook. I'm sure she'll be happy to show all her lady friends at the retirement village."

Caleb growled. God, he hadn't thought about his mother and all her cronies seeing it. "I never figured you to be so considerate. Anyway, thanks, bro. See you later."

"Oh, before you go…"

"What?"

"When's the happy day?"

"What happy day?"

His brother did a rendition of the wedding march over the phone. A really bad one. Caleb rubbed his brow, which was really starting to pound.

"There isn't going to be one." And most definitely not now.

"What? I got the impression from Richo that you and this artist are pretty tight."

"You know I'm done with the ball and chain route. Once bitten, twice shy, and all that. Get it through your head, she's a friend, that's all." *Though now, not even that.*

"A friend who paints you in the buff after what looks like it must have been some pretty hot sex."

"So I'm a good actor."

"Good thing, because you're a shit liar."

"Goodbye, Dylan."

"Hey, don't be like that. You're my baby brother! I'm worried about you, that's all."

"I stopped being your baby brother when I beat you in

that hundred metre race in year six, remember? So go worry about something else." He killed the connection before his brother could further extend the inquisition and went and dug out his favourite road bike.

He wanted to push himself and feel the burn in his muscles from a gruelling hills ride, but the roads were still scarred and littered with debris from the fire, and besides, it would take him closer to the woman who didn't want to see him, so he turned his road bike for the beach. Fast and furious would have to cut it.

He pushed himself hard, dodging parked cars and orange Metro buses as he pedalled hard down Magill Road towards the city, the cogs in his mind turning just as fast.

He'd always been lucky with the girls. He and Dylan had had fun pretending to be the other and playing tricks on the girls who'd never seemed to mind. Both the Knight twins were considered catches.

So lucky. Then he'd met Angie when a hairdryer at the hairdressing salon where she worked had shorted and started a fire, and he'd fallen hard and fast and he hadn't give a damn about whoever his brother was dating after that, Caleb knew he'd found the one. He'd thought himself the luckiest man alive two years later when Angie had said, *"I do"*.

But apparently his luck had run out about then, because Angie, who'd married him knowing he was a firefighter started whining whenever he was on night duty or had a callout, telling him she could never make plans and it was no kind of life in which to bring kids into the world.

A truck roared by, spewing out diesel fumes. Damn right, it stunk. She'd known what kind of life it was before they were married, and he'd been staggered to think that somehow she'd just assumed he'd have a change of heart and decide to get some kind of boring desk job.

That's when she'd given him the choice. The job, or her.

The sad thing was, by that stage, it hadn't been hard to choose.

The heavy city traffic thinned on the other side, and he powered down Henley Beach Road toward the coast.

He'd thought his luck had changed for the better when he hooked up with Ava. A dream arrangement. No commitment, no ties, and the bonus was no whining about night shift or coming home stinking of smoke. Just hot sex and plenty of it.

He caught his breath in the salt tinged air at Henley Square, chugging water and munching on an energy bar as seagulls squawked overhead while he stared out over the summer beach scene with the long jetty over the turquoise blue sea of the Gulf.

He sure hadn't meant to blow it by falling in love.

Dickhead.

He turned his bike for home, powering hard against the slight gradient towards the foothills where he lived, pushing himself harder until his muscles burned and his mind was blank and, for just a moment, one blessed moment, he could forget what he had lost.

ONE DAY AT a time, Ava told herself while she cooked up a batch of red curry paste, refusing to give in to the sadness of knowing she'd never see Caleb again. She'd heard it took twenty-one days to break a habit and it was barely seven.

Through her kitchen window, she could see the world turning reddish gold under the westering sun. Inside, the air turned pungent with spice and heat as she ground the chillies, garlic, and spices in her pestle. She had a food processor somewhere in her cupboards that did the job in a fraction of the time, but today there was something satisfying about physically grinding the ingredients, pulverising the toasted cumin and coriander seeds, pounding down the lemongrass and galangal until the smooth paste came together. All she had to do was persist and be patient and it would come together.

Just like all she had to do was hang on, and day-by-day, this hollow ache in her soul would subside and pass.

But there was a peace there too, as if baring her soul and speaking it aloud had released the log jam of self loathing. Nothing could change her past, but the truth was out there. It was almost as if the gorge's eucalyptus scented air had swept inside her aching soul and chased away the darkness.

Oh, it had lost her Caleb, but it was better this way. One thousand times better to let him go now. One thousand times better than to incur the savage slash of betrayal. She knew all too well how that felt. She was never going back to that dark place again.

Even if it meant a little pain now. That was all it was.

It would pass.

In time.

Chapter Eleven

ONE SHIFT ROLLED into the next and February rolled into March. Nominally autumn, though that didn't mean the mercury couldn't still reach dizzy heights and that the threat of bushfires was over. There would be no end to the bushfire season until April thirtieth, and only then if there had been good solid rains and the bushfire threat had dropped below severe. Only a few years back they'd had a bushfire in the Adelaide Hills in May. Ridiculous, once upon a time, but after a string of dry years, there was no reason the bush couldn't burn given half a chance, no matter what the month.

But for now the weather had moderated, temperatures hovering in a band between the mid-twenties to mid-thirties Celcius. Perfect weather for sitting on your ass at home watching telly. *Not*. He didn't want to spend yet another night doing that.

"You wanna come to the Maylands tonight?" Caleb asked Richo, as they changed into civvies at the end of their shift.

Richo grinned. "Not likely. I've got a date with Gillian. We're taking in a show at the Fringe before heading out somewhere for dinner."

"Oh." So he was still seeing Gillian. Well, at least something good had come out of Ava's exhibition. Not that it helped Caleb. And he'd already learned Tina and Matt had plans when he'd asked them. It seemed everyone else in the world was getting shagged.

"Mate," Richo said, shaking his head and with a hand on his shoulder. "You've got to get out more. There's a whole Fringe Festival going on out there. Mad March in Adelaide, and you're sitting around looking hangdog all the time. You've got to get over her, and the only way to do that is to put yourself out there. If I were you, I'd be carrying that newspaper clipping of you and that painting around in your back pocket and showing every chick in the bar. They'll be falling over themselves to tear your clothes off."

"Thanks," he said, for what was probably good advice, except he didn't want just any chick at the bar. He wanted Ava, except she didn't want him.

Pointlessly, he checked his phone again. Nothing. He hadn't heard from her in two weeks. That probably meant he could give up on this pathetic hoping she'd be changing her mind. That probably meant it was final.

Yeah, Richo was right, he ought to get over her.

If only he knew how.

AVA DROPPED INTO the blessedly cool air of the gallery ten minutes early for a scheduled "Morning Tea with the Featured Artist" session, to find half the two dozen or so seats already taken and Evan brimming with excitement. "I've got two pieces of good news for you," he said. "Twenty-four of your pictures have sold! How's that? And there's still a week of the exhibition to run!"

"That is great news," she said, needing the boost to her spirits more than she'd care to admit. She'd never been a fan of the meet the artist type sessions where for an entire hour and a half she had to pretend that, instead of being the introspective painter who liked to work alone, she had to perform as Ava Mattiske, the outgoing artist, who loved nothing more than doing a Q&A on her art and influences. She would much rather her art speak for her.

Besides, it was so hard to appear fresh and interesting, especially now when she was having trouble sleeping properly at night. "What's the second bit?"

"I'm not telling you." Evan winked conspiratorially, waving to the women who had just entered the gallery. "Not until afterwards. But you're going to love it, I promise."

"Oh, okay." She saw the women sitting down. "I might just get a glass of water."

"Ava? Are you all right?"

She put a hand to her temple where a dull ache throbbed in a vein. "I'm not sleeping well. It's the heat."

"You don't have air conditioning?"

"Just a fan." *Spinning around and ultimately going no-where.* She hadn't turned it on since that night.

"Take your time. I'm sure your audience will wait. And then the really good news, and I promise you're going to feel a lot better."

It was two hours before the last of the audience had ceased with the questions, and left, two hours of studiously not looking in "that" corner where a certain picture was hung, although there were also two more red dots on her pictures by then, so the session had been worth it.

"It's the Federal Department of Agriculture," he said in a conspiratorial whisper after the morning tea attendees had given their thanks and were gone. "They want to commission you, for an entire series showcasing Australian fruit." He mentioned a figure that was their starting point and her mouth fell open.

"You're kidding me?" A commission like that would pay her way for the best part of a year, but not only that, would get her art in front of the entire country. Who knew where that could take her?

"You need to talk to them, Ava. And you seriously need to get an agent," he told her, nodding. "You don't want these offers being communicated through me. I can't help you like an agent could."

"I know," she said, knowing in her head what he said was right, but she couldn't bring herself to commit. Who to trust when she'd gone so wrong before? "But thanks so much for fielding the enquiries."

"Oh," he said, as she was on the way out. "And your fire-fighter friend's picture is up to three thousand six hundred dollars. How good is that?"

She glanced towards the picture she'd been avoiding all morning, of Caleb looking magnificent all spread out on her bed, and felt a stab of pain in her heart so sharp, it made her catch her breath. She moved towards it numbly, drawn to it. Alongside it was pinned the cutting from the newspaper.

"Very good," she said softly, drinking in his perfect form with her eyes, wanting to reach out and touch his skin and feel his warmth again.

"Will you tell him?"

"Who?" she said, wondering at the pain inside her, this pain that wouldn't go away, that left her numb and listless and puffy-eyed come morning.

"Caleb Knight, your model."

She snapped her eyes away. "Oh. Look, he'd probably love to hear it from you. Why don't you give the station a call?"

She left a quizzical looking Evan in her wake, together with a phone number to call the marketing director of the Department of Agriculture and a reminder to find herself an agent. Still buzzing with the good news, Ava stopped on the way home to pick up her mail from the local post office. As usual, there wasn't much, a couple of window envelopes from the bank, another from her energy provider, but there was one in a fancy white envelope, her name and address type written on the envelope, while the stamp said it was from Singapore.

She slit it open and a notecard slid out of a folded paper.

And what she saw on the notecard turned her blood cold. *Her name, in her mother's handwriting.*

She recognised it even now, even eighteen years on, it was still enough to put a shiver down her spine.

What the hell did her mother want? Now? After all these years?

She put it back down and circled it for a while. She poured herself a glass of wine and sipped at it while she stared from all angles at the envelope and the note card sitting alone on the bench top. Her mother had abandoned her to hell. And even when Ava had reached out, her mother had told her there was no choice.

Like an unexploded bomb, it sat there. And in the end she couldn't bear it. She had to reach for it and rip it open. She unfolded the small notecard determined to tear it in tiny pieces if it dared begin with "Darling daughter" or even "Dearest Ava". But it started with neither. It began with two other little words. "I'm sorry".

And Ava's knees buckled and she collapsed onto the sofa.

'I cheered for you the day we heard you had escaped.' it read. 'I wished you wings to fly. I wished you the freedom I had never been strong enough to seek or to fight for. I wished you the happiness that was stolen

from you. I wished you love.

'I hope you have found all of these things, and more.'

Ava blinked as she read the words her mother had committed to paper, of how she had watched her career blossom from afar and how she'd provided for her, and instructed her lawyers to send this letter, after her death.

'I know I will never have your forgiveness,' her mother had written in conclusion, *'and neither do I deserve it, but wanted you to know, I'm so very proud of you, Ava.*

'I wish, I so wish things could have been different.'

For a long while Ava sat there, holding the letter, the words blurring in her mind, as she thought back, searching for a hint that she'd missed, a clue that her mother had felt something for her.

And all she could find was the memory of being rocked in her mother's arms, being told not to cry, that tears made eyes puffy and men liked their women to look happy and beautiful, and Ava didn't understand. She couldn't understand. Not when she could see tears welling in her mother's eyes too.

She put a hand to her mouth. Because there too was the memory of her mother taking her out one day, shopping, she'd told her husband, and Ava had imagined coming home with new gowns and underwear and designer shoes in preparation for another party and another man, only for her mother to take her to the zoo of all places, and they'd wandered around the grounds, looking at all the animals and eating ice cream and laughing, and it had been so unexpected and joyous.

And she remembered her mother brushing her hair, the long brush strokes through her hair like a caress, when Ava had fallen and sprained a wrist.

Tiny glimpses of kindness amongst the dark, and none of it had made sense.

Her eyes fell on the abandoned envelope, the letter still folded inside. She reached for it, unfolding it, the black legalese print stark on the white page. Her mother had provided for her, it said, and there was a number, an unimaginable number attached to that clause. Her money now.

Ava sucked in a breath, and took herself to the windows overlooking the gorge and beyond and put her hand upon the glass, solid and yet invisible, like the ties that bind people together, even when you she couldn't see them, even when you she thought they were severed and cast away.

The ties that bind you forever.

And the air shifted around her as the heat haze shimmered over the horizon and the cold, withered heart inside her chest started beating again, and nothing was how it was before.

Because the freedom her mother wished for Ava and that she'd thought she'd found was another kind of prison, but this time self-imposed. She hadn't embraced her freedom. She'd become trapped inside it, afraid to live. Afraid to love.

Lights flashed along a road in the suburbs below, red and blue speeding out of sight as soon as they'd appeared, and a stab of pain in her chest made her gasp.

Caleb, she thought, her fingers curling on the glass, before she pushed herself away and headed for her studio.

She found her sketch book where she'd left it in the studio, while pencilling some herbs, a bunch of basil and coriander and rosemary she'd picked from her herb garden. She flicked through the pages until she found them, the original sketches she'd made of Caleb, the first right here in this studio, of him pulling on a shirt, in the shower with the water cascading down his corded throat and over his muscled chest and sprawled on her unmade bed.

She collapsed onto her sofa, her fingers tracing over the lines, wishing it was his body under her fingertips, wishing for his heat and his strength and the warm masculine scent of him, the sense of loss growing until it threatened to swallow her whole.

Caleb, whose only crime was that he loved her.

Because she'd been too stupid to realise what was staring her in the face the whole time. That she loved him too.

She flung the book aside and put her head in her hands.

What the hell had she done?

Chapter Twelve

CALEB WAS BACK working nights, the February fire a thing of the past, and everyone hoping that summer had thrown its worst at them, when the incident came in at four in the morning. A string of brush fence fires in the leafy eastern foothill suburbs, disturbingly close to the Uriarra Gorge.

All available units were called out, the high winds and tinder dry conditions pushing panic buttons all over the emergency services, none pressed harder than Caleb's.

His appliance screamed its way to their callout, arriving to find his worst fears realised, the residents in the street were all out desperately trying to wet down their houses with garden hoses because what had been started as a malicious prank by some idiot, was already spreading fast through the bush of a neighbouring picnic area. Some of the crews got to work on getting the residents clear and ensuring the houses were safe while more chased the fire in the trees that was being fanned by the wind and heading directly towards the gorge.

The crews fought desperately to get a handle on the fire, to control it before it could get into the gorge, everyone knowing that if it got there, into the steep and heavily wooded terrain, it would be impossible to stop.

As the battle progressed, Caleb's gut knotted tighter and tighter. It was a race against time, a race against a fire rapidly gaining the ascendancy and heading for the gorge, the flames metres high above the treetops, dancing from tree to tree, to a soundtrack of crackling roaring fire. He pulled out his phone, not caring if Ava never wanted to hear from him again, she was going to.

There was no answer. He knew the emergency services would be sending out warning messages to everyone in the area but that didn't stop him from sending off his own text. *Fire coming. Get out now!*, before he got back to work.

When it was clear there was no stopping it this end, they sent crews around the flanks, bouncing up the rough fire tracks around the gorge to try to get any residents in its path out of the way. Caleb's appliance was one of them, climbing about the burning valley below, grey and white smoke billowing upwards in massive clouds, turning the dawn to dusk. But, from his vantage point here, he could see the path the fire would take, and knew there was no way it could miss her.

He could just about make it out, a ridge or two away, the low stone house set into the side of the hill, the big rain water tank on the side. Had she activated the sprinkler system yet? Did she know what was coming? "There's Ava's house," he called. "Let's get her out."

They were through one rocky dip in the track and over the next ridge, when Richo said, "Shit," pulling the truck to a sudden halt.

Before them a massive gum tree had fallen across the track, the diameter of its trunk a couple of metres at least. No way around it, and no job for a mere chainsaw when there was fire raging through the gorge.

"We can't get through this way. We'll have to go back."

"No!"

"Caleb, there's no way. We have to turn around and try to find a track in from the top."

Which was when Caleb had jumped out of the truck.

"What are you doing?" yelled Richo.

"Go," Caleb yelled back, already scrambling his way over the fallen tree. Because he knew a way that didn't rely on the roundabout fire tracks. He knew it from what felt like a hundred years ago when he'd played amongst these hills and gorges with his brother, and he knew that even on foot he could make it this way before the fire front when a vehicle never could make it all the way around in time.

And because now that he was this close, he wasn't about to leave Ava stranded.

"You're bloody mad, you know that!" Richo called after him, even as he was reversing the big truck around. "They'll chuck you out of the service for this dumbass stunt, if you bloody survive, that is."

Caleb just waved them away, already finding the path through the bush that he'd once known so well. Richo was probably right, but right now he Caleb didn't care about the job. All he cared about was getting to Ava. And getting there in time.

The path was overgrown from how he'd remembered it, there were more fallen trees to clamber over and inside his suit he was a soggy, sweaty mess. But below him the flames lapped at the edges of the gorge and he kept right on going.

SHE WOKE TO the smell of smoke. *Fire.* Outside her windows the view had turned grey. Fear clenched her gut. She found her phone, realised it was still switched off for her session at the gallery yesterday – so stupid – and flicked it on. Meanwhile she sprinted to the pump box on the side of the house to get the sprinklers working, messages pinging into her phone one after the other, telling her to activate her emergency fire plan or get out from the emergency services, one from Caleb telling her the same.

The wild winds whipped at her hair, the smoke was terrifying, ashes already falling from the massive dark clouds belching from the gorge, the noise fearful, roaring and crackling. The fire was enormous. She was no hero. She'd never planned to stay and defend on her own. She'd turn on the sprinklers and get the hell out and if the house was still standing when she got back, well and good.

A new message popped in then, another one from the emergency services, telling her it was now too late to evacuate, and to activate her survival plan.

Oh, god.

"Stay calm," she told herself, her heart racing, her fingers tangling, fumbling with the key to the pump, one eye on the monstrous orange glow from below, the roar of the fire making her want to get in her car and go, and not stand here trying to get this damned pump to work.

It took her three attempts but finally it started, the pump kicking in and sending water cascading over the roof and under the eaves. Would it be enough though, given what was coming? She slammed the pump door shut and turned, just as something emerged through the smoky haze. A figure in yellow and running, trying to shout something over the roar of the fire. She narrowed her eyes, when a sizzle of recognition zipped down her spine.

Caleb!

He glanced over his shoulder at the gorge below, at the flames now visible in the treetops across the gorge and yelled at her to get inside. But she was already heading towards him, she wasn't going anywhere without him. He caught her up and got her by the hand and tugged her forcibly through the wall of water and inside the studio. "Get to the safe room," he ordered, as he pulled away anything flammable from near the windows. "Now!"

She managed to grab her sketchbook on the way and another small canvas she'd been tinkering with.

"What about that one?" Caleb asked behind her as they rushed past the mad painting of herself as a teenager on the bed.

"Leave it," she said, and they fled into the tiny retreat room at the back of the house and slammed the door, huddling down near the floor. It was dark, the power gone, and there was no way to know what was happening outside, no way to know anything other than Caleb was here.

And it felt like her heart was beating a thousand times a minute, she was so terrified, but she had Caleb's chest for a pillow and his arms to hold her safe and she hung onto him for dear life.

The noise intensified, like a jet flying directly overhead, the temperature in the tiny room soared, and she buried her face in his chest and swore that if she ever got out of here alive, she was never going to send this man away again. From somewhere outside came the sound of smashing glass and she jerked in his arms. He squeezed her tighter, but that wasn't what forced the tears from her eyes as the noise retreated, the roar abating.

"You came for me," she said, trembling in his arms, clinging to him, as the enormity of all that had happened in the space of just a few minutes set in. "You risked your life for me."

"I had to," he said gruffly, still panting from his exertions.

"I love you," she said.

He stilled. "What did you say?"

"I said, I love you."

"Jeezus, Ava, you sure pick your moments," he said, but there was a chuckle underlying his words. He lifted her hand in his glove and kissed the back of it. "I love you too. Now come on, we've got work to do."

The fire front had passed, but not the danger, and together they worked for two hours in the blackened exterior, putting out spot fires and watching for flare ups. Her car was a burnt out mess, and she shivered when she thought about how close she'd come to getting in and driving away. But the house had survived, the sudden drenching protecting it from the fire, the only damage to the house was the glass wall of her studio and the contents lying scorched and broken on the floor.

She looked at what was left of the picture of her lying on the bed, nothing more now than a charred canvas painted by fire, and she was glad.

Caleb put his hand on her shoulder as she stared down at it. "We could have saved it."

She shook her head. "That frightened girl is gone," she said. "She turned one prison into another, locking herself away. I'm never going to allow myself to be frightened again."

She turned to him and took his hands in hers. "I'm sorry

it took me so long to see what was right there all the time. I fell in love with you, Caleb, without even realising it. I'm sorry I sent you away. I'm sorry I hurt you."

"And here was me, thinking I must have imagined you saying those words while we were stuck in there."

She shook her head. "No, you didn't imagine it. I worked it out yesterday." And she told him of the note from her mother, written long ago, and that she could never ask for forgiveness, but wishing Ava freedom and happiness and love. She told him of the scattered fragments of memories, of kindnesses she'd buried so not to disrupt the perfection of her dark past.

He listened to it all, and he pressed his lips to her forehead, smelling of smoke and ash, his face grimy, "I love you," he said.

"I thought nobody would, if they knew the truth. And I was too afraid to believe it could be true."

"Believe it," he said, a finger under her chin, angling her for his kiss. "It's true."

"I love you, Caleb."

And he pressed his lips to hers and he tasted of ash and fire and the flames of love he had stoked in her heart.

THEY WERE OUTSIDE, Caleb taking an axe to some burnt saplings, when the truck pulled into the driveway.

"Bloody hell," Richo said, climbing down from the cab

to slap his mate on the back. "Are you a sight for sore eyes?"

"What were you worried about?" he lied. "I had heaps of time."

The relief on his crew's faces was palpable, and it was a very celebratory reunion as Richo radioed in to tell base they'd found Caleb safe and well.

"So what's the latest with the fire?" he asked, nodding in the direction of the smoke cloud that seemed to be growing smaller by the minute. "Did it get anywhere near Reynolds Ridge?"

Richo took off his helmet and wiped his grimy forehead with the sleeve of his jacket, leaving another smear of grime in its place. "Nah, not even close. It's caught up with the February fire ground and run out of fuel way short. Lucky, eh? A bit like you."

And Caleb sighed with relief. This day could not get any better, unless…

He pulled Ava against him and kissed her brow, before he took her hand in his and ducked down on bended knee. "Ava, I love you. Will you marry me?"

"What?" Richo said, looking on. "Get out of here."

"Shut up," Tina said, with an elbow to Richo's ribs.

Ava blinked down at Caleb. "You're not serious?"

"Marry me, and let me love you forever."

"Marry him, and put him out of his misery," urged Richo.

"Shush," said Tina.

Ava laughed. "You really mean it."

"Of course, I mean it."

"Then, yes, I will marry you."

And Caleb pulled her into his arms and spun her around. "We're getting married," he said, "and you're all invited."

And there were whoops of joy all round.

Epilogue

June

THE WEDDING WAS timed for the weekend following the annual National Firefighters' Conference being held in Adelaide this year, which gave them an entire week to celebrate not only the upcoming nuptials, but all of the romantic developments that had happened in the Knight family since they'd last been together.

Ava was feeling slightly overwhelmed. Together, with Caleb, they'd shown everyone around the hotel function rooms of the Stamford Grand Hotel at the Adelaide beach-side suburb of Glenelg where the wedding and reception were to be held the following weekend, before they'd headed to the cocktail bar to celebrate. Tonight it was standing room only, the generous seating nooks with their big leather chesterfields, cosy sofa booths and bar side seating alike, all overflowing with the after five crowd. In the corners of the ceiling were hung massive screens showing tonight's AFL game between the local team, the Crows, and Melbourne, though if anyone could hear the commentary it was a miracle over the buzz of conversation, with the Knight group in one corner out all noising the rest, though it was fair to say it wasn't Ava who was responsible.

Ava was too busy trying to keep up. Dylan and Hannie she'd met previously when the two couples had gone out for dinner together, and she'd taken an instant liking to the woman who would marry Caleb's twin brother, Dylan, who looked so much like Caleb and yet not quite, a slightly different flavour of the same DNA. The Knight cousins and their partners had flown in from Brisbane and Melbourne today, and now she sat tucked up on one of the chesterfields between Caleb on one side and Dylan, who had his arm draped around Hannie's shoulders, her arms crossed at the wrists on her knees, one ring amongst her chunky silver rings sparkling in the lights. Adjacent to them sat Logan, tall and broad-shouldered like the rest of the men, and Arabella, or Bella as she preferred to be called, with her choppy bob of blonde hair and gorgeous blue-green eyes, while on opposite sat a very pregnant Darington, or Dare as she told Ava to call her, her long body nestled with her feet up on the sofa against her fiancé, Lachlan, who preferred to be called Lock. If Ava managed to keep any of their names straight, it would be some kind of miracle.

"Who would have guessed it six months ago?" Logan said, raising his beer to the group. "All four of us hooked up and heading full steam towards the state of wedded bliss within the space of half a year." He shook his head.

"And nobody," Dylan added, "would have taken bets that my little brother, he who had sworn off marriage for life, would be first cab off the rank."

Beside her, Caleb growled, but there was a smile underlying it. "You only got a ten-minute head start, bro, because I move a whole lot faster." He squeezed Ava's shoulders and smiled down at her and Ava was warmed by the love in his eyes. "And with good reason."

Lock coughed. "Well, I hate to burst anyone's bubble, but you're not actually going to be the first cab off the rank." He wrapped Dare's hand in his as he smiled over at her. "We've already tied the knot."

"What?" yelled three Knights in unison.

"When was this?"

"When were you going to tell us?"

"Why weren't we invited?"

Lock laughed and held out his hands. "Settle down, you lot. Dare and I made it official while we were back with Dare's family in the States in March. We were planning on doing it again over here sometime."

The first beer coaster hit him smack in the middle of his forehead. "You bloody better," said Caleb.

The second thwacked him on the ear. "Bloody nerve, not even telling us," said Dylan.

The third knocked over his glass, spraying what was left of his beer down one leg. Logan laughed, along with everyone else. "Bloody well deserved that too. Reckon it's your shout, you secretive bastard."

"It's funny," said Dare, in her soft southern accent when the laughter and the ribbing died down again. "It's almost like Leonard was sprinkling fairy dust down on us all the day of the memorial service."

"Who are you calling a fairy?" said Lock, putting his hand on her swollen belly. "How do you reckon these two got in there, divine intervention?"

"Please," said Logan, holding up one hand, a look of distaste on his face. "This is getting perilously close to being too much information!"

"And this is a family show," agreed Dylan, nodding wisely.

"Indeed it is," Caleb said, clutching her hand in his. "What do you reckon, about your new family, Ava? You reckon you can put up with these turkeys?"

Surrounded by four fine specimens of the masculine kind where broad shoulders and chiselled cleft chins abounded, and shirts and trousers moulded to every movement of muscle beneath, it was like sitting in the midst of some kind of testosterone soup. Even the pregnant Dare, angular and strong featured, with her shock of platinum hair in a closely cropped style, exuded power and strength, while the other women, she thought, lent the broth sweetness and spice, not to mention a whole lot of bling given the number of engagement rings on show, and made it whole.

She smiled at them all, soon to be her new family, or a

part of it at least. Caleb had warned her about all the various uncles and aunties and the thirty to forty cousins heading to Adelaide next week for the celebration, the concept of such a huge family unknown to her with numbers that made her head reel.

"What I want to know is, is everyone in the Knight family as buff as you guys?"

"They wish," said Dylan.

Dare snorted. "Not likely."

Logan just folded his arms behind his head, making his shirt buttons cling on for dear life, and laughed.

"Then, seriously, I'm honoured to find a place in this family, and I want to thank you all for making me feel so welcome."

The group cheered and toasted Ava and the soon to be wed couple, after which the toasts kept right on coming. For Logan and Bella, for Dylan and Hannie, and for Dare and Lock who had beaten them all to the punch line.

"Oh," Dare said, her hands clutching her belly.

"What's wrong?" said Lock, frowning beside her, ready to spring into action.

She sat herself up, stretching out, her black tube dress clinging to her baby bump. "Your babies are kicking up a storm in there, that's all." And they were and for a moment the group was enthralled, watching the moving skin-scape of Dare's belly under the stretch fabric of her dress.

"It's the footy," said Caleb, looking up at the screen. "I

reckon you've got a couple of potential Crows players there."

Lock growled. "Carlton, more like."

"We ought to toast these two," said Logan, lifting his glass again. "To the two newest members of the Knight clan."

So they raised their glasses again and then they raised them to Leonard, because even if he hadn't sprinkled fairy dust down on them from on high, long ago together with their grandmother, he'd sure set the wheels in motion for what was happening now.

Caleb's round was next so he took himself off to the bar and Lock went to give him a hand while Dare, Dylan, and Logan took a bathroom break. Then Hannie decided they needed some food to go with all the drinks and took Bella in search of dips and fries, leaving Ava to mind the seats.

It was densely packed at the bar and Dare was back first. She sat herself down next to Ava, her athleticism obvious in the way she controlled her descent, even against a shifting centre of gravity. "It drives me crazy, I swear. I managed all of ten drops, yet the way my bladder was pressing on me, I was expecting Niagara Falls. You're an artist, I hear," she continued without missing a beat. "My mum is an artist."

"Really? What kind?"

"Visual. Sketches a lot of life stuff."

Ava nodded. "I get that." Right now she was itching to sketch Dare's face. Up close, her features were even more striking, the high and wide cheekbones, the straight line nose and the arched brows over aquamarine eyes, and then the unexpected lushness of her mouth in the midst of all those angles. "I bet she loves drawing you."

Dare gave a very unladylike snort. "Don't worry, she's got much more interesting stuff to sketch. I saw the picture you did of Caleb, Dylan passed it on. You're good. And, uh"—she looked around, only continuing when her eyes fixed on Caleb and Lock, just starting to make their way back from the bar—"who knew my cousin was quite so ripped?"

Ava laughed. As far as she could tell, all the Knight males were ripped and, aside from her baby bump, Dare was obviously keeping herself fit and toned.

"Dang," she said, her hand on her belly, "here we go again. I swear these little guys are going to kick their way out. I don't know if I can take another nineteen weeks of this. Mind you, kicking their way out is probably preferable to doing a John Hurt on me."

"Who?"

"Oh, you know, the guy in *Alien* who gets infected with the thing growing inside him?"

Ava must have looked blank.

"Oh, well, you probably wouldn't want to think about having babies anyway, if you had seen it. Though there are times I wonder if the way it isn't supposed to happen naturally isn't worse. Ooh, that was a big one." She looked over at Ava. "Do you want to feel them moving?"

Ava was shocked. To put her hands on Dare's bump seemed almost an act of intimacy and she'd only just met the woman today.

"Here," said Dare, making the decision for Ava, taking one of her hands and placing it against her belly.

The fabric was warm against her skin, warmed by the body beneath, but as for movement, she waited and could feel nothing. And then came a cluster of kicks, the staccato beat like a series of firecrackers going off, followed by a movement that felt like one of the babies had stuck out a knee or an elbow and tumbled over right under her hand.

She blinked up at the woman. "Amazing." It was all of that and more. It was wondrous. And then it went quiet under her hand and she took it away.

"Are you and Caleb planning on having kids anytime soon?" Dare asked, reaching over the table for her glass of water. "It'd be great if our kids could play with your kids, when we could get together that is. Melbourne's not that far from Adelaide, only an hour's flight."

"I don't know," Ava said honestly. "We haven't talked about it." He knew she had doubts and he understood why and he wasn't asking anything of her what she wasn't sure she could give.

"I didn't want kids," Dare continued. "At least, I didn't think I did. Then these two happened along and now I can't wait to see their faces and hold them in my arms. Funny how things can change when you least expect it, huh?"

And Ava thought about the dark place she'd been, and of the loneliness of her self-imposed isolation, and how now it was like living in a lighted world, where there was so much to experience and so much to feel, and thought, wasn't that the truth?

Caleb and Lock returned, bearing two trays filled with drinks and a fresh jug of iced water for Dare, the muscles under their rolled up sleeves clearly never off duty. And as Dare got up to head back to Lock, an idea started forming in Ava's mind.

"You look deep in thought," Caleb said, as he plonked himself down next to her in the seat Dare had just vacated. "Penny for them?"

"I don't know. I was just thinking that when I sketched those pictures of you, I had no idea that there was a whole battalion of Knights who'd look so good on the page."

"Damn straight," said Logan, returning to the group just ahead of Dylan.

"Yeah, and way more deserving than Caleb too," his twin said, banging his fist against his chest. "We know you must have needed a barrel load of artistic licence with that one. Time for the real deal."

Ava smiled, loving the competitiveness between the brothers and their cousins, loving the way they could bag each other when it was clear that respect ran deep. "I'm already itching to sketch Dare."

"Really?" She looked at Lock. "Wow, that'd be so cool.

But when?"

"Why not this week while you're all at conference? It's not like our wedding isn't already organised, there's nothing to do but wait now until the big day. Do you guys have to be at the conference all day every day?"

They all looked at each other before Dylan spoke first. "There's a couple of sessions I don't need to be at." Dare and Lock looked at each other and agreed.

"And me," added Logan. "Once my presentation is out the way Wednesday, I'm home free."

"But what would you do with the pictures?" Lock asked. "Do we just hang them on a wall when they're done?"

"I don't know. Maybe auction them like Caleb's? Raise money for charity? What about the Bushfire Appeal?"

"A calendar!" Caleb said. "Featuring all of us. We could be the next firefighter calendar, not with photos this time, but sketches."

"But no buttocks," Ava promised, really getting excited now. If there was something that got her enthusiasm going, it was a new creative project, and she felt that same zing of energy she'd felt when she'd hit on sketching Caleb's back. "You'd have to have your pants on at least."

Dylan shook his head. "But there's not enough of us for a full twelve months."

Ava counted them off on her fingers as Bella and Hannie returned. "But there's Caleb, Logan, Dylan, Lock, and Dare, and I could do one with both of them too, so that's half the year covered."

"I can round up a few of the troops," Caleb said. "I reckon Richo will be in like Flynn for starters. I'll talk to Mike, our station manager, see what he reckons, whether it'll work. But I can't see why it wouldn't."

AVA HIT THE ground running. Caleb rounded up his crew, so she had Matt, Tina, and Richo, and even Mike put up his hand, and Dylan pulled in a couple of his crew to make up the twelve.

It was a very rowdy bunch that got together the next Friday night in the cocktail bar after the wedding rehearsal, waiting to check out the sketches, cheering as each was revealed. There was Caleb bare chested, thumbs hooked in his low slung pants, and Dylan kneeling on the ground with Hannie's Labrador sitting between his legs. Dare was standing hands on hips and wearing a bandeau over pants, the licking flames of her bold tattoo embracing the smooth tight round of her baby bump. A bare chested Logan balanced an axe in his wide grip, while Mike struck a blow for the fifty-somethings, square jawed and stern, the curls of his chest hair greying on a body surprisingly buff, though Caleb searched for him to see his reaction and saw he wasn't there – he'd slipped off to one side, pressing his phone hard to his ear.

One by one the sketches were revealed to cheers and applause but it was the picture of Richo that got the most laughs, posing with a hip height spraying hose.

"What?" he said, his arm tight around Gillian on his lap, when Tina snorted.

"I've spoken to headquarters," Mike said, back with them after the last picture had been revealed and the laughter and cheers had died down, "and I want you to know they're behind this project one hundred percent as a fundraiser for the Bushfire Relief Appeal. Ava's going to work up the finals and then it's off to the printer."

More cheers and clinking of glasses ensued. "There's only one thing left to decide," he added, "and that's a name for the calendar."

"Beefcake on Parade!" yelled Dylan.

"Firing Up," suggested Matt.

"Richo with his Favourite Thing," called Tina, and the mob descended into fits of laughter again and even Gillian laughed this time.

"I've got a suggestion," Ava said, when the laughs died down, for once having no trouble figuring a title for a collection. "I think it should be called Brothers Forged in Fire, because even if you're not a Knight or don't have the tattoo, isn't that what you all as firefighters are?"

It was unanimous and there were cheers all around.

It took five minutes for the din to die down before Mike raised his hand and asked for silence again.

"But headquarters had some even better news they want

me to share with you all. The results of the investigation into last year's Victorian bushfire has just tonight been released – and drum roll please, because, as we damned well knew should be the case, Leonard Knight has been exonerated of all charges!"

Everyone was up cheering and back slapping then, the Knight brothers and cousins and their firey mates and even the soon to be Knight women.

"To Leonard Knight!" cried Caleb in the midst of the din, holding up his glass.

"To Leonard!" everyone toasted, and the legend lived on.

LATER THAT NIGHT Caleb was standing behind Ava on the balcony of their suite overlooking the ocean, his arms wrapped lovingly around her body, and if there was a chill in the air, neither of them felt it. Tomorrow they would be married here, in the ballroom overlooking the beach while tonight the sky above was inky blue, a big moon sending a ribbon of gold across the ocean. Meanwhile, a big corner spa bath was filling in the en suite.

"You really are something special," Caleb said. "Clever. Gorgeous. Not to mention sexy as hell." He leaned down and pressed his lips to her throat, breathing in the lemon scent of her hair, his hands scooping low around her hips, his thumbs edging close to her sex.

She made a sound like a purr, and angled her head to

give his mouth free reign. "I do believe the feeling is mutual."

"You know the guys are all crazy about you. They already were, but you've really won them over with this calendar idea."

She turned in his arms, slid hers around his neck and pressed her lips to the vee of his open shirt, squirming her hips closer against his growing hardness. "I like your family. They're very…" She kissed his chest again and then pulled his head down and kissed him hard, sucking him into her hot mouth.

He growled his approval. "Very what?"

"Hot. Like you."

He was getting there, his temperature rising along with an erection that was growing harder with every beating pulse of his blood and a need to be inside this woman that was damned near combustible. "I'm seriously thinking it's time we took this inside."

"How's the spa going?"

"It'll do."

"Is it bad luck to make love the night before your wedding?"

"I'd say it would be bad luck for the both of us if we didn't."

She smiled up at him, the moonlight lighting up the highlights in her hair, matching the golden flecks in her cognac eyes, not waiting to move inside as she got to work unbuttoning his shirt. "That's the right answer."

They peeled their clothes off each other as they went, and made it to the bath almost naked, desperate for the touch of skin against skin and the slide of flesh against flesh.

"Perfect," he said, testing the water.

"Almost," she said, scooping rose petals from a bowl and scattering them on the surface, the rose perfume released and rising in the heated water.

"I'm going to come out smelling like a flower," he protested.

"No," she said, "you're going to come out smelling like me. If you play your cards right, that is."

He growled and dragged off what was left of her underwear, testing her slick folds, finding them incendiary as he discarded his own in the rush to get her into the spa after him. He pulled her astride him. Her breasts bobbed on the water, her dark nipples an invitation to his mouth and his swirling tongue, while her core teased his tip, rocking him against her swollen clit.

Until he pulled her down hard as he drove into her and she gasped and cried out and it was like their first, frenetic time together again, except this time it was better, because this time it wasn't just a moment, this time was a taste of forever.

Afterwards, on the bed where he'd finally bundled her, he pressed his lips to the tattoo on her back. "This is you," he said, "my phoenix, reborn and strong."

"You have a lot to do with that."

"No, you did it, Ava. You had it in you all the time. You pulled yourself from hell and made yourself new again. I'm so proud of you." He traced the lines of the stylised phoenix on her shoulder and saw her eyelids flutter closed.

And then she spoke. "I can't forgive her, you know. I don't think I ever will. But I feel like I understand her more now. She was a prisoner too." Then she gave a long sigh and opened her eyes. "I was speaking to Dare about the babies."

His fingers stopped where they were on her skin. "Oh?"

"She let me feel them move. It was incredible. I felt them tumble under my hand. So tiny, but already so strong, and I didn't want to say anything then, but I've been thinking ever since..." She pressed herself up on her elbow and looked evenly at him. "I wondered if I could do that? After all that's happened, could I be a mother? I mean, a good one?"

"Oh, Ava," he said, reaching for her hand, pressing his mouth to the back of it, "I've seen you with children. You love kids and they love you. You'd be the best kind of mother."

"Do you really think so?"

"I know so."

There was moisture in her eyes and he reached up with the pad of one thumb and gently wiped it away.

"I think I'd like to try, that is, if you wanted to. I think I would like to have your babies."

He felt moisture dampen the corners of his own eyes

then, and it was no wonder, as his heart swelled so big for this woman, there was no room for anything else inside his chest. He slid his hand behind her head, lacing his fingers through her hair. He'd never thought himself a poet, but he felt himself coming over all William Shakespeare right about now.

"You know how much I love you, Ava? Do you know how long I will love you? I will love you to the ends of time and I will still be there for you, wherever we are, whatever we are. We'll be together forever. I promise you."

Ava smiled, her eyes bright. "I love you, Caleb. Thank you for teaching me how to trust again. Thank you for teaching me not to be afraid of love. Thank you for not giving up on me, when, by rights, you could have walked away."

He wrapped an arm around her shoulders and pulled her towards his mouth. "I'm never walking away from you, Ava. Never. Trust me on that."

"I do," she said, testing out the words she'd need tomorrow, before his lips met hers and his kiss told her it was true.

The End

The Hot Aussie Knights

Headed by grandfather Leonard (The Legend) Knight, the Knight family is fire-fighting royalty in Australia. Two generations have followed in Leonard's highly distinguished footsteps and nowadays, despite being scattered across the length and breadth of Australia, it's the five Knight cousins who keep the Hot Aussie Knight legacy alive, working hard and playing hard, day and night.

Book 1: *Hot Mess* by Amy Andrews

Book 2: *Burning Both Ends* by Sinclair Jayne

Book 3: *Long Hot Summer* by Victoria Purman

Book 4: *Burning Love* by Trish Morey

Available now at your favorite online retailer!

About the Author

USA Today Bestselling Author, Trish Morey has written thirty romances for the internationally bestselling Harlequin Presents line and her stories have been published in more than 25 languages in 40 countries worldwide, including being published in Manga comic book form in Japan, and as Trish Moreyova in the Czech Republic. Trish was awarded Romance Writers of Australia's Romantic Book of the Year Award (the Ruby) for short, sexy romance In 2006 and again in 2009, as well as being a finalist in the Romance Writers of America's prestigious RITA Awards in 2012. A qualified Chartered Accountant by trade, Trish was employed as financial manager at a major business school prior to her first sale.

Trish lives with her husband, 4 daughters and assorted menagerie in the beautiful Adelaide Hills.

For more from Trish, visit TrishMorey.com.

Thank you for reading

Burning Love

If you enjoyed this book, you can find more from all our great authors at TulePublishing.com, or from your favorite online retailer.

Printed in Great Britain
by Amazon